BURDEN OF TRUTH

BURDEN OF TRUTH

SEQUEL TO AFTER THE GREEN WITHERED

KRISTIN WARD

Daughter of Erabel Series

The Girl of Dorcha Wood

Blood of the Lost Kingdom

A Storm of Wrath & Ruin

Young Adult Dystopian Series

After the Green Withered

Burden of Truth

Young Adult Fantasy

Rise of Gaia

Burden of Truth

By Kristin Ward

This is a work of fiction. Names, characters, businesses, places, events, locales, and incidents are either the products of the author's imagination or used in a fictitious manner. Any resemblance to actual persons, living or dead, or actual events is purely coincidental.

Copyright © 2018 Kristin Ward

All rights reserved. No part of this book may be reproduced in any form or by any electronic or mechanical means, including information storage and retrieval systems, without written permission from the author.

Independently Published

Editing: David Taylor, thEditors.com

Cover: JD Cover Designs

ISBN: 9781731253170

I love you, Mom. I'll miss you forever.

PROLOGUE

I can still feel the weight of the dead child in my arms. The memory of the slackness of his muscles after the last breath rattled out of his chest, lingers in my brain. His sightless eyes continue to stare at me when I am alone, and I know that I will never cease to feel the burden of their gaze.

I deserve to feel it. It is a stain on my soul I must carry.

Before all this began, I had no true understanding of the world beyond the border of Prineville, my small town in the Pacific Northwest Basin. Like many others before me, I had accepted life under the control of the Company, though I had secretly harbored dreams of living outside the barbed boundaries. But those were empty fantasies, wispy things with no substance. I know better now.

My hometown seems like a distant memory these days, clouded in hazy recollections and indistinct feelings.

So much has happened that I am at a loss to pick up the pieces and put them into some semblance of order and normalcy. It is as though that period in my life happened to someone else, and all I know is the after—the world of recruitment, training, and killing.

My journey into the underbelly of my world truly began with my assignment as a Pathfinder. Covert missions led to startling truths as I was thrust deeper into the web encompassing the Drought Mitigation Corporation, or what most of us refer to as the Company or DMC. Then, in the bowels of Renascence, a micro-city within the walls of Brigford, I stumbled upon a secret the Company had kept hidden, evidence of something so profound that to reveal it would shake the very foundations of our society.

The DMC is creating a new form of human, reared in seclusion and secrecy. This mutation, born out of countless trials and tragic errors, is being bred for a purpose, one that feels foreboding. Like so many others, I assume that I have become one of the expendable, while those cosseted few are provided a world of opulence compared to what lies beyond their safe borders. The remaining masses, undeserving wretches, struggle for the scraps they are given and plod through life in a haze of despaired acceptance.

However, there is leverage in my knowledge. I have been given an opportunity to reveal what I know and rip away the veil that shrouds the power that controls us. But it has come at a great cost.

The resistance, those hidden freedom fighters that embody my thirst for truth, offered Springer and me a place within their ranks. It is a bold move, an irrevocable step that will put me on a path against an enemy who will stop at nothing to see me captured and killed. But there have been too many sacrifices to stop now. There is too much that can no longer remain hidden.

What is salvation?
Is it the hand
that reaches into
the dark depths of your soul
and pulls your humanity
out of the mire?
Or is it the swift death
of a perfidious dream?

CHAPTER ONE

There have been so many half-truths and dodged questions over these many months. Springer keeps a part of himself at a distance, always shielding me from the whole truth. I have acknowledged these omissions without giving in to my resentment, but inside I've railed against the knowledge that things have been hidden from me. That time is over. The curtain has lifted, and I am free.

No longer will I remain blind to what I have become. While I accept that I allowed myself to be shaped into a weapon, molded by hands that once held me and shared my visions of a better future, I can now use my training for a greater purpose.

Springer and I were assigned to monitor and identify rebel factions infiltrating a food processing and storage facility. The purpose was to eliminate all but one. The survivor was to be captured and interrogated. This is not how the assignment ended. No one survived, and it was within this series of events that I finally found the strength to turn my back on all that I had been taught and trained to do. When the moment came for me to decide, the choice had already been made.

I have become what I have hunted: a traitor.

Springer and I leave the food processing plant to find a secluded spot outside the perimeter. Driving the Company jeep beyond the compound, under the guise of surveillance, allows us to hide from prying eyes that watch our every move and ears that strain to hear too much.

I find the air easier to breathe out here, though I know it's just an illusion. I may be beyond the patrolled fence, but I am never truly outside of those invisible barriers. My hand absently rubs the microchip embedded under the skin of my inner wrist. The reminder of their omnipresence keeps the fires in my heart burning as we continue on. I need this anger. It builds my strength and hones my purpose.

Being contacted by a rebel faction—and offered the chance to finally learn the truth—prompted Springer to let down his guard and take me on this journey. I am on the cusp, a precipice as daunting as it is exhilarating. I know he will finally tell me everything that he's kept hidden, around it. But if there is truth in this, then what does that mean?

His voice interrupts my internal battle. "After Bram was recruited, he moved through the ranks quickly and was placed under the watch of an individual in the intelligence sector. I don't know the specifics, but Bram began to work for both sides, methodically developing his reputation within the Company while also ensuring that his connections extended to the other side."

Springer pauses, looking at me to gauge my reaction. I'm unable to do anything beyond sitting there, listening to this inconceivable story, so he continues. "You have to appreciate how dangerous this all must have been, and all the while, he kept an eye on you and bided his time until he could get you under his wing. When the recruitment period in Prineville arrived, Bram made his move."

I lean back, letting the truth sink in. "Are you telling me that Bram turned me into a monster, intentionally? I've *killed* people, Springer! Children! Their blood is on my hands. That's not something I can just accept and forget. You don't walk away from something like that. And now...now you're telling me that Bram orchestrated it all? That he took me from the only home I've known and put me on a path to become what I abhor just so I would see some truth?" I feel a wrenching in my heart, as though it has been torn all over again.

"Enora, you have to underst-"

"No! I don't have to understand anything more than

Bram turning me into a murderer just so I can come to some realization of what he already knew." I start pacing, my anger flooding my muscles, making me feel feverish. Oh, God. I knew Bram was somehow a part of all of this, but finding out that he's so coldly moved me around on some insane chessboard of his own design makes me sick. I stop moving when another thought enters my mind. "Could he have stopped Safa from being arrested?"

I almost fear his answer when I hear his voice softly reply, "No. That was out of his control."

I nod jerkily. This is so much to take in. "This makes me hate him."

Springer gives me a small smile of understanding. "He knew you would, but he had faith in you and hoped that you would find your way and be able to face the truth of the world you live in."

Turning around to face him, I say, "Was it worth the cost? To him, I mean."

"This is a war, Enora, and in a war, there are losses on all sides."

"That's so heartless."

"I don't think Bram can afford to consider it any other way."

All I can think is that the heartless soldier Springer is describing is not the boy of my childhood. That boy wouldn't have seen the killing of children as a necessary consequence of this war. "Why didn't you tell me all of this before?" Inside I keep thinking maybe it would be easier to accept if I knew the rationale behind it.

"I couldn't." I make a face when he says this. "Enora, you have to understand the risks in all of this. Bram never wanted your life put in danger or for you to see the ugliness of this world, but he also didn't want you to end up stuck in Prineville, never knowing what it is that you are working for. When you and I began this journey, I had my doubts about your ability to execute this role and potentially see the Company for what it really is, brutal in its control. I wasn't sure you could handle it, and I didn't know if you would continue to believe the lie even when faced with the truth."

"What truth was I meant to see? That the DMC is not some benevolent power protecting us? Did he want me to see that I've believed the lie all my life, like some kind of mindless robot?" I think about those children whose blood is on my hands, and I want to wipe my palms on my slacks in an effort to rid myself of it. But there's no changing what I've been a part of. And Bram brought me to this point. My anger and hurt overwhelm me.

"He turned me into a killer!" My eyes fill with tears, and I shake my head to fight them off. "He turned me into a killer just to teach me a lesson. I don't understand this. He knew me so well, and to put me on this path where the blinders are ripped away with every evil thing I'm a part of is cruel. That's not how he treated me when we were young. He was always there, looking out for me. Until he was gone." I turn my face away, focusing on some distant point in the dull landscape.

"There are some things he can't protect you from."

I know Springer is right, but I fight that knowledge. I sit back down, shifting my legs to rest my head on my knees. "Was I supposed to find out that the Company's true goal is to make some super-human?"

Springer shakes his head. "Bram didn't know about that. No one in the resistance did."

"How can that be? I mean, here you are, telling me that I've got this pitiless-fairy-godmother type who's been funneling me along in some awful maze until I find what he's been hoping I would see! This is so wrong! Why didn't he just tell me?"

"If he had, what would you have done?"

He's got me there. Being told something is much less effective than seeing it with your own eyes. But I've done so much more than just watch it all happen from the outside. I've been the hand that wields the weapon, the hand that pulls the trigger. I hate that Bram wasn't honest with me, but that emotion pales in comparison to the rage I feel at having been molded into something I am not, rather something I was never meant to be.

I suddenly feel weighed down by all of this. My hands cup my head as images of Bram and me up on a hill, snuggled together and talking about a future that could never be, are overlaid by blood and cold calculation. This new knowledge hurts.

but I find it comforting to know that we are not alone in our efforts.

And this brings me back to my anger toward Bram. In my heart, I know that he couldn't have shown me any of this without putting me into my role as Pathfinder, specifically Springer's Pathfinder. My participation in this is an evil I am meant to accept.

"How did it all begin for Bram? Did it start back home or only after he was recruited?"

"I don't know, Enora. Honestly, I never asked, and I doubt he would tell me anyway. Being ignorant of the inner workings of what he's doing is a necessary precaution. If you or I were caught and interrogated, the less we know, the better."

"Yeah," I agree, but where does that leave Bram?

We sit in silence.

Bram's smart to keep things close and protect everyone he can. That's the part of him I knew and loved. So I can't find fault with his purpose, just his means. But if I'm honest, I must acknowledge that there may have been no other way for me to come to this point without having seen and done all that I have.

I look back and think about how everything has brought me *here*, to a group of people who will stand against a power that seems indomitable. Bram used his position to get me out of a town that would've eroded my will and swallowed my identity. He threw me into a life that is tainted with experiences I wish I could erase from my mind. Yet he also gave me a chance at another path, one he put before me but left me to choose.

Bram forced me to experience it all to determine how to use the information I learned. He gave me a small piece of freedom called choice. It is a cold reality that so much in my life has been predetermined, even discovering the truth. I've done terrible things to get where I am. But I can hold no lasting resentment toward Bram for directing my path to this point. I do, however, ache to know the potential repercussions of his choices.

The next day, having received some communication from Bram, Springer informs me that we have an assignment on the outskirts of the processing plant. I can see from his expression that this is just a ruse, and my heart accelerates at the prospect of making physical contact with 'traitors'. Throughout my life, I have been conditioned to view those rogues outside the town limits as dangerous conspirators, enemies of the country. Even now, I have to be mindful of the flares of warning that surge into my brain. These are part of the lie. I must face the truth now.

We leave the compound, heading in the opposite direction as yesterday, though the landscape all looks the same to me. Having been provided with some specifics, Springer drives to exact coordinates. We arrive in a small depression and see desolate countryside covered with abandoned buildings. The structures look like broken skeletons. It's disturbingly quiet as we pull to a stop. Nothing moves. There is no breeze, no flap of a curtain in the broken windows, no birdsong or hum of electric motors once ours is shut off. The heart of this place stopped beating long ago. We exit the jeep, and I spend some time just slowly walking through this ghost town, looking for something, anything, that would indicate recent human activity.

There is no fence here, no border to keep anyone out or anyone in. This must have been one of those towns that were gutted when the large absorbed the small, back in the old days when the world went mad. It's an eerie feeling to walk through the empty streets. Layers of dirt cover everything. The buildings that remain lean sideways as though drunk on the desolation of this place. We stop at what must have been the center of town. There is a broken fountain among rusted picnic tables that sit vacant, like the rest of this place. I look over at Springer.

He shrugs and says, "I guess we wait."

I let out a frustrated breath. I'm not sure what I was expecting, but I admit that I did anticipate a form of welcome. Instead, this just feels deflating after having built up the moment of arrival in my mind. After a while, I kick a rock in frustration, stubbing my toe in the process, and spend a couple of minutes hopping around and turning the air blue while Springer just laughs and shakes his head. I scowl at him when the pain begins to subside and limp over to a cement bench that survived the years of neglect.

My anger gets the best of me as Springer continues to chuckle. "Yeah, really funny. You're such a hero, standing there laughing at me." I slip my shoe off, and dirt comes spilling out of it.

This just makes Springer laugh harder until he finally pulls himself together. "No one suggested you play soccer with a rock." Apparently, he's a comedian because this sets off another series of spastic laughs.

"You're an ass." I rub my toe and do my best to ignore Springer.

The minutes pass, and he joins me on my perch, slinging his arm around me. I elbow him and call it even. It feels good to laugh. It's been so long since we've been in an atmosphere where we could let down our guard. I smile as I think about how it could be once we officially join this contingent of rebels. It's so easy to visualize a future peppered with carefree days. As these visions play out in my imagination, I can picture Bram here with us. It could be like old times.

Ten minutes later, we hear a soft rumbling. Turning toward the sound, we watch in fascination as a patch of soil, just outside a large building that is one of the few still standing, splits and folds back, tucking itself under previously unseen rims on the surface. What's left is a large rectangle leading below ground.

It seems clear that we were likely being watched the

entire time we were waiting. Standing together, Springer and I make our way slowly to the opening, giving each other small looks that communicate our wonder and unease. No one emerges, and we end up standing awkwardly in front of the large manmade hole. It gives me an odd sensation to look into the depths. I give Springer a glance and follow him onto a ladder that is barely visible from our vantage point. We descend into darkness.

Guns are trained on me the moment my feet touch bottom. I look over and see that Springer has his hands up, though he's calm, unruffled by the severe looks we're receiving. They are a suspicious lot, these rebels. Their skin is sallow, which only accentuates the gauntness of their features. Food is scarce, as is sunlight.

While I stand there, trying to take it all in, a sour stench registers in my brain. My nose wrinkles in distaste as the scent assaults me. The smell is some noxious combination of body odor and human waste. I take a step backward without thinking and bump into the metal ladder. It takes an act of will to regain control and breathe normally. The last thing I want to do is piss these people off. They seem edgy enough already. In the back of my mind comes another thought, viral outbreak. Visions of newscasts plastering warnings about the X3 virus run through my mind. I can't help wondering if there is a mixture of virulent particles in the air as I breathe in the rank staleness.

I take a good look at their threadbare clothing in the dim light. The pants and shirts donning each individual are more like a collection of patches than any whole item. I wonder how often the original garments had been worn and passed down before being too tattered. Everything must eventually be relegated to a rag pile. That is obviously where their clothing has come from.

Under the shirts are arms that are too skinny and bellies that cave inward in painful thinness. I feel self-conscious standing there in my spotless uniform and well-fed body. My hands drift to my shirt, plucking at the fine fabric. I tell myself my clothes are just a mask. Not long ago, I, too, wore shirts sporting holes and felt pangs of hunger at all hours of the day. I wonder now what I must look like to these people. They must think I'm a drone.

"What are your names?" A woman's voice sneers.

I find her pointed face a couple of people over. Like the rest, she's got her gun pointed at us, though I sense that she wouldn't be too put out if we made a move, giving her an excuse to fire it.

"I'm Springer, and this is Enora. Commander Bram Williams sent us to these coordinates. Sergeant Murdock should be expecting us."

"I don't see why your kind would be welcome here." The woman snaps.

"Back off, Nola," a young man mutters while lowering his weapon. "Trevor, take them to headquarters."

I look over at the person he's referring to. He appears young, though his face is marred with scars of deep craters across his forehead and cheeks. I wonder at the cause.

"Follow me," Trevor says in a voice that cracks at the end, reminding me of young boys going through puberty.

We're led into a subterranean labyrinth. The cement and metal floors, with numerous platforms and ladders, have a musty smell. This mixes with the already nasty odor of this place to create a new, more repellent stink. I'm thankful for the poorly lit passageways. I wouldn't want to look too closely at anything I'm walking on or brushing against.

As we walk through the dimly lit tunnels, Springer strikes up a conversation with our escort in an attempt to learn more about this group. "How long have you all been down here?"

Our guide through this underworld, a teenager from the gangly look of him, turns to Springer and shrugs. "Not sure exactly, but I was born here."

I can tell this doesn't surprise Springer. He must have assumed as much, but I'm rather appalled to think of children growing up underground, scurrying about like rats.

"How many people are here?" Springer asks.

The boy, because I can't in any way refer to him as a man, cocks his head. "I'd say about fifty. There were about twice as many before the outbreak a couple of years ago, but that took lots of us, most of the adults."

Only fifty? It's such a small number. My heart sinks with the knowledge that everyone would know the individuals we killed in the food processing plant raid. They were essentially a family. It also means that those killed would've been a big part of this tiny population. Hearing about the viral outbreak also explains why they were so very young. It is a sobering thought, and my mind curls upon itself as I sink into deeper silence, consumed by anger and guilt.

By the time we reach an underground juncture, we've easily walked a few hundred feet through the earth. I look up at the web of shafts extending in varying directions, some even deeper into the ground, and wonder at their initial purpose. They look vaguely similar to those in Renascence, but I note many differences too, making me think that this structure was not originally intended as a sewer or water system. So many more metal platforms and ladders lead deeper into this vast system. In my mind, I imagine how far some of the offshoots might lead and whether they end near large towns or cities.

Springer and I are shown into a small room and told to wait while our guide jogs away in lanky strides, as only the young do.

I look over at Springer. "What do you suppose this place was built for?"

He glances around the room, likely envisioning the portions we just traversed. "I'm not sure. From the look of the offshoots and rooms like this, it seems like it was some kind of underground bunker." I nod and consider what that idea implies. "In fact, I would wager that this particular section is not even in the heart of this facility."

If that's true, then it seems that the Company would

know about this place and within that thought is a high element of risk. "Wouldn't a bunker like this be known to the Company?"

"You would think so, but if they knew about it, then this would've been obliterated long ago," he replies with his typical certainty.

"I guess you're right. It just seems so unlikely that this would be undiscovered after so many raids."

"Not necessarily, Enora. The old pipeline you found at the food processing plant wasn't linked to this facility, so this may have also gone under their radar."

But it still seems highly unlikely to me, and I can't help the seeds of suspicion from rooting themselves into my subconscious.

Our conversation stops once the door opens, admitting what appears to be a high-ranking official. Springer and I jump out of our chairs and watch as a man enters the room with an air of authority. Like the others we've seen, he has pale skin stretched across a face whose cheekbones are painfully prominent. While his uniform is less worn than the others I've seen, he still looks shabby next to us, and this makes me feel like a spotlight is shining on my perfect pants and pressed shirt.

His gaze briefly takes us in before extending his hand in welcome. "I'm Sergeant Murdock."

Springer and I take turns clasping his cool grip before Murdock indicates that we should return to our seats. He pulls a chair up in front of us and sits back before saying, "I want to thank you both for agreeing to meet with me. I understand the risk you are taking and will make this brief." He looks at Springer and me for confirmation and continues. "As you are now aware, we have been in contact with Commander Williams for quite some time. This is the only reason why you find yourselves among us. The commander has done a great deal on our behalf, though his most recent actions have put us at a severe disadvantage."

I want to cringe when he says this, all too aware that Springer and I have killed more people than this tiny group can afford to lose in this small faction of fifty. But, I don't know what to say and settle for a quiet, "Yes, sir."

He looks sternly at me, and I want to squirm. "It is a huge loss. But in this war, there are many losses. Without Commander Williams' assistance and others like him, we would find our efforts completely obstructed, leading to even greater damage to the resistance. I have asked you here because we have been made aware of intel from one of your assignments. If what Commander Williams says is true, this information could be a catalyst for our work."

Springer sits forward, elbows resting on his knees. "I can assure you, sergeant, that what we discovered could have a profound impact on your supporters and those who are blind to the truth."

Murdock smiles thinly. "That is good to hear. While I am eager for the full report, I have been informed that

Commander Guire would like to be in attendance when you both review the data you gathered from Renascence."

I'm a bit surprised by the idea of delaying, and I admit that I'm also disappointed. I have held onto this secret for what feels like ages, and the urge to open my mouth and let it out is nearly overwhelming. But I manage to clamp down on the impulse and sit in quiet obedience.

Springer, ever the diplomat, responds to this news. "We understand, sir, and look forward to the opportunity to explain our findings to you and the commander."

Murdock inclines his head in appreciation and then turns to me. "I understand that you, Enora, were the one to discover our access point to the food processing facility. However, the outcome of that particular operation is not one I had anticipated. What can you tell me about that?"

His question takes me off-guard. I hadn't expected to be asked about what occurred, what we did, and it makes me squirm to have to talk about something that affected everyone in this dark place. My throat feels dry. It always does, but now I feel my tongue sticking to the roof of my mouth, and I struggle to scare up enough spit to swallow and clear it. When I compose myself, I launch into a brief recounting of the events of that night and the subsequent video analysis that led to my discovery of the abandoned underground system outside the perimeter of the facility. Throughout my explanation, Murdock sits back and listens without emotion, aside from a brief flicker of pain and anger when I gloss over the deaths of those who had infiltrated the food storage room. When I finish my retelling, the room is enveloped in silence. I look away from Murdock's gaze and focus on the floor, waiting for him to break the stillness.

Finally, he says, "It seems that we were not as careful as we should have been." I neither agree nor disagree, feeling like his statement is laced with accusation. "And the video footage?"

"It has been erased, sir."

Murdock nods in approval before stating, "I assume that you can return to the Company in your former capacity."

Springer responds quickly. "Yes, sir. Our roles are intact. We can return to our base once we indicate that this assignment is complete."

I can tell that Murdock is pleased we will continue our roles and thereby act as informants. "Then you will be our eyes and ears as we move forward with our operations. And I trust that your movements from this point forward will not result in further losses on our side."

The warning is clear. While Bram has been doing his part to fight for the rebels, Murdock cannot run the risk of losing more people. In a place of a mere fifty individuals, the losses they experienced must seem astronomical. It can't be easy to keep this band going, and I feel incredible remorse for the impact we've had. This is just another example of how Bram's cold calculation has left blood on my hands. This group of fighters has only been able to survive by infiltrating food facilities with the help of people on the inside like Bram. But for me to fully understand the evil of the Company, we were tasked with killing some of the very people we want to join. I wonder if everyone here knows what we did. I think they must. Do they understand that we had no knowledge of the hands manipulating our way to those killing grounds?

There is no need to ask of our willingness to be part of this, just our promise that we will do what we can to minimize casualties. It feels like a promise I can keep, but I've been deceived before.

As Murdock briefly outlines the next stages in our collaboration, I experience a strange sensation running through my body. I have felt pulled in various directions by unseen forces that have controlled my actions for so long. Now, I feel the strings of my marionette body cut, one piece at a time.

Snip...snip...snip.

Returning to the food-processing center following our meeting is a tense time. I keep looking over my shoulder as we make our way through the building, thinking that at any moment, I will see a troop of guards bearing down on us. But Springer was right. Our deception is undiscovered. I know that it is Bram we have to thank for that.

To wrap up our assignment, we fabricate documents indicating that the individuals who were eliminated were a small, family group living in the tunnels just outside the perimeter of the compound. In my report, I cite multiple breaches of food storage over a period of time, lending credibility to our work. In reality, these raids have happened on a steady basis to feed the group of rebels living outside DMC control. As I think about this, it makes me wonder how they will continue to survive.

Springer detonates a gas bomb in the shafts that would kill any living thing that may have remained hidden to reinforce our lie. Of course, we had planned this with Murdock prior to our return to ensure that no one would be in that underground system. I feel some measure of relief when the head of security at the plant thanks us and submits a report to our commander, Bram, indicating that we have found and eradicated a rebel force. As we leave the compound, I look back at the structure and marvel at how it could look the same as when we entered, yet now everything is different.

CHAPTER THREE

The success of my recent assignments has finally paid off. On our return to the training center, I find myself given quarters in Springer's housing unit. Of course, I know Bram's hand was in this decision and that he expects me to use my newfound autonomy to my advantage. But I relish the comfort and seclusion as I stretch out on my new bed for the first time, staring up at the ceiling and replaying the many events that have brought me to this point. So much has happened. So much has changed. I have changed.

As memories flip through my brain like snippets of video, Safa's face enters my mind, and I freeze the image, holding onto it. Where is Safa? Is she still alive? And if she is, is she whole? I want to ask Bram about her. He must be able to use his contacts to find out her whereabouts or if she lives. But part of me is afraid to ask. I may not like the answer.

Having been granted increased communication privileges, I place a video call to my parents that evening. It's good to see their faces when the call goes through. They look fit and healthy, unlike my childhood memories when they were gaunt and disillusioned.

"Enora!" They exclaim when they see my face.

"Hi, Mom. Hey, Dad. It's so good to see you both. How are you?"

"Oh, honey, we're doing so well these days! You know, ever since your recruitment, we've been able to do so much more, and it has made our life here much easier."

I can see the effect their new status has had in every smoothed line of their faces. "I'm so glad to hear that, Mom. You both look really good!" They turn and look at each other and chuckle. I don't recall the last time I saw either of them laugh.

"Do you know that your dad and I have even been able to buy some new clothes? Do you remember ever being able to do that when you lived here?"

"No, I can't say that I do. All of my clothing always looked worn the day we brought it home. I know how you feel, though. It's how I felt when I got my uniform. Before then, I'd never had anything too nice."

"And you look so grown up, Enora." My mom's voice loses some of its distinctness as she prattles on about this and that. My mind drifts.

Listening to their chatter illustrates how my position within the DMC has impacted their lives in ways I hadn't foreseen. It gives me pause as I think about the repercussions of my recent contact with the resistance. Won't the Company go after them if I am found out? Will they be considered traitors by default?

I've been half-listening until I hear my dad ask, "Honey, are you okay?"

"Huh? What do you mean?"

"You just seem distracted and worried about something. Is everything all right over there?" Of the two of them, it's always been my dad who is most in tune with me. It hurts a little to lie to him, but I know I can say nothing to explain my feelings. This call, any call, to them is being watched.

I try to smile. "I'm just exhausted. There's been a lot of work lately, and I just got back from a long assignment. I need a good night's sleep, that's all."

To alleviate his worry, I add, "Hey, I got moved up into better quarters. I've got my own room now, and the food is amazing. I get so much food and water that I've got extra at each meal. Can you imagine?"

"I'm so proud of you, Enora." My mom says with a sincere smile on her usually sour face. "You've done so much for all of us, and I'm glad your efforts are being rewarded. This placement with the DMC is the best thing that's happened to our family."

It's hard to hear that. She doesn't know the truth about

the Company, and I can never tell her. I can only hope that my work with the rebels will reach my parents and that they will finally understand it all. I hope they don't hate me when they realize I'm a part of it, when they figure out I'm a traitor.

"Thank you, Mom. I'm so glad you both are doing well. You look great!" And they do. But now, I worry about what the future holds for them.

"You get some rest, honey. Okay?" My dad leans into the camera when he says this, probably his way of emphasizing that I must listen. I chuckle, but it sounds fake to my ears.

"Yes, sir. I love you both. We'll talk again soon." I blow them each a kiss and pretend to catch the ones they send my way, and then I cut off the call.

The excitement of meeting with the rebel forces has obviously clouded the potential ramifications to my family. To be honest, until today, I hadn't given a thought to the consequences to them. It shames me to think about how callous that is.

But would I change my course of action if I know they will be punished? No. I can't go back. All of this is so much bigger than my family. By stepping back and taking a hard look at this choice, I finally see why Bram has manipulated my way to this point. To him, the gain outweighed the cost. I am making the same choice. So, how can I blame him when I am forced to be just as ruthless?

.   .   .

I AM TAKEN ENTIRELY OFF GUARD WHEN I SEE BRAM for the first time after our return. He is making his usual sweeps of our unit and enters the room where Springer and I are cleaning and prepping our equipment for whatever assignment awaits us. I feel my heart stutter when he walks in. Where before I suffered only feelings of betrayal, I now feel a wealth of emotions I am hard-pressed to interpret. There is anger and resentment. But this is tempered with love and appreciation for what I know he's sacrificed and why. I see more than the calculating soldier standing before me. Beneath the layers of control and manipulation is a man fighting for the greater good.

My entire body seems to vibrate, wanting to spring up and run into arms that once held me in the innocence of my youth. But, somehow, I reign in the urge and give him a shaky smile instead, knowing he'll be able to read my face like an open book and see all that I must leave unspoken.

Bram looks into me, eyes reflecting an understanding and love I had never seen before. But his voice projects none of this. "Enora, I received your report and am impressed with your work on your last assignment."

I can't trust myself to speak. I bite my inner cheek to stem the flow of words I want to say and simply give him a curt nod. There are always eyes watching and ears listening. I know this is the reason for his formality, but I want to fling caution aside for a protracted moment. I want to rage at him for turning me into a killer. I want to tell him I love him. I want him to know I understand.

It's Springer, always Springer, who rises and walks toward Bram to shake his hand in appreciation of the compliment. "Thank you, Commander Williams. Enora showed great ingenuity, and we were able to efficiently deal with the problem."

"I do not doubt that you both performed above expectations. I wanted to discuss another mission in an outlying area, a few miles from your last assignment. I would like you both ready to leave within the week." Springer nods before Bram continues, "You will come to my office for specifics this afternoon."

"Yes, sir."

Bram looks down at me once more as I sit anchored to the floor to keep myself under control and gives me a soft smile. "Enora, I know that your continued work will be a tremendous benefit to all of us."

The implication and underlying message in his words are unmistakable. I clear my throat, intent on being able to express some of my thoughts, even if they are shrouded in formality. "Thank you for your faith in me."

He mouths 'always' and walks out of the room.

Two days before Springer and I head out on our next assignment, one that I know is concocted solely as a means to make contact with the resistance, I run into

Drake in a hallway of my new housing unit. I look into his handsome face. It's hard to imagine that his open expression truly hides something menacing, as Springer had been so adamant to convince me of. I'm suddenly not so sure. Could Springer have been wrong? Was my misgiving just a reflection of unfounded warnings? Drake's grin is so boyishly disarming as it splits his face, there is no way I can remain unaffected.

I smile back. "Hey, Drake. I haven't seen you in so long!"

"Enora!" He exclaims and reaches toward me, pulling me into a warm embrace.

I lean back automatically, the closeness of his arms wrapped around me taking me off-guard. He reads my body language, and lets go. I can't help noticing a shadow of something pass across his face. When I've put a little distance between us, I ask, "How are you?"

"I'm good. Lina and I just got back yesterday."

I try not to make a face when I hear her name. I've been unable to set aside my anger at having been betrayed by her when Drake and I met in secret. She's such a typical drone, picture-perfect on the outside and riddled with ugliness on the inside.

Drake watches me and says, "Yeah, I know how you feel about her."

I grimace. "Sorry. I just don't trust her. Of course, she's not as bad as Nero. That guy is like some super-drone, always looking for an excuse to be an asshole."

"Oh, I bet you haven't heard about him."

"Uh, no. But now I'm hoping you're going to tell me he's been kicked out of the program or something like that."

Drake laughs, shaking his head. "Sadly, no. But he didn't cut it in a specialized program, so they shipped him off to some food production plant north of here. Most likely, he's just a typical Sentinel over there."

I feel somewhat mollified by this news. "It's not the best outcome, but I'm glad he's not around here anymore. I bet he was pissed when he found out." I can't help the grin that lights up my face at the thought of Nero hearing the news. He deserves it. That guy was a snake.

"At least it means one less drone around here," Drake tells me, always eager to use my term for the elites who plagued my life in Prineville. "Lina's been a good partner, even though she acts all high and mighty sometimes."

"I don't know how you put up with it day in and day out, Drake. I can only take her type in small doses."

He looks away. "Well, let's not talk about her then. So, how have you been? What sorts of assignments have you and Springer been given?"

I'm a little taken aback by his question. He must know that I'm not supposed to give specifics, none of us are, and it makes me uneasy having him ask. "It's been good."

Drake rolls his eyes. "Really? That's all you can tell me? Enora, I hope you know that you can trust me." He leans in as he says this, as though trying to convey his sincerity with proximity.

Springer's warning briefly flares in my head, like some parental advice alert lurking in my subconscious, and I tamp it down. I look hard at Drake, at his perfect face. I want to trust him. But I realize that regardless of whether he's honest or not, I must play along. There is too much at stake now.

"You're one of the only people I *can* trust, Drake." But the words feel oily in my mouth.

He reaches across the distance and strokes my cheek. I close my eyes and live in the moment, trying to listen closely to my intuition. As I do, I realize this doesn't feel right. Springer's words whisper in my head... *he's using you.*

"Will you meet with me tonight?" Drake's voice drips with feeling.

I close my eyes tighter, racking my brain for an excuse to put him off. "I want to, Drake. I'm just scared. I've got new quarters now, and I don't want to risk losing that privilege if we get caught."

He chuckles softly. "I get it. You just don't want to lose that soft bed you've been rewarded with, right?"

Relief fills me as he plays along. "Well, duh! After months of sleeping on a bunk in a room with a bunch of girls who would sooner spit in your face than talk to you, would you?"

"Not when you put it that way!" He smiles, but I can

see the gears turning. "You know, you don't have to worry. I've got a new place for us. It's not even in the dorms. It's in our housing unit, actually."

I can't help the surprise on my face at this news. "Are you in the same building as me now?"

"Yep. Lina and I got our new placement when we got back. I guess we've impressed Commander Williams too."

This revelation doesn't sit well with me. If Drake truly is using me, this placement has given him more access to my whereabouts. I hide my feelings and jokingly say, "So, what you're saying is that you moved up faster than I did, huh?"

"You know, now that you mention it, I guess I did." He gives me a teasing look, but there's a hint of something more in it.

"I'm glad you got your new quarters, and I promise I won't hold it against you that you got rewarded so quickly." I playfully punch him in the shoulder and start to turn away, hoping he's forgotten about wanting to meet with me in secret. But he's tenacious.

"Considering we're so close to each other now, it'll be easier to get away."

I turn back and fidget, trying to find the words that will convince him to back off on the idea. "I can't. I mean, I just got settled, and Springer and I are prepping to head out in a couple of days. I don't want to risk it."

"Come on, Enora. It's been weeks since we've been

together. You can't imagine how much I've missed you," his voice needles me.

I can see the pleading in his eyes and am not immune to it, but I strengthen my resolve and shake my head. "No, Drake. If we get caught, it would be awful. I can't. I can't do that to Bram." The second I say it, I want to suck it back in. I watch Drake's face as he takes in that little comment, and my heart sinks when he makes a connection.

"Bram?" There is a long pause before he finishes his thought. "Do you mean Commander Williams?"

I want to wring my hands. That was so stupid! I can't believe I said it. I try to cover up the slip by saying, "Yeah, the commander. He's the one who decides who gets to move up, right? I'd still be stuck in the dorm if he hadn't determined that I'd earned better housing."

"You called him Bram. Do you *know* him or something?"

"Of course, I know him. He's our commander." It sounds so lame the moment I say it. And Drake won't let it go.

"That's not what I mean." There's something unpleasant in his voice, something he may have hidden before, but it is there now.

I try to play it off, but it's like a runaway cart I've let loose. There's no way to get it back. "I don't know what you're saying."

"Oh, don't you?" There's a sneer in his voice, and for the

first time, he looks ugly, as though some inner thing has emerged, eroding his outer perfection. "So you won't meet with me anymore, but you'll cozy up to *Bram*? Is that how you ended up going into fieldwork so much faster than me? You been laying on your back for him, Enora? Trading favors?"

I flinch at the insinuation and take a step backward from what I see creeping across his face. "That's disgusting, Drake." I turn to stalk away in anger, but he lunges after me, grabbing me from behind, snaking his arms around my body in an immovable grip.

"Let me go." I spit at him, rage flooding my muscles.

"Oh, I don't think so," his voice whispers in my ear, hot breath moving across my neck. "I don't think you get to tell me what to do." His left hand slowly shifts, reaching for my breast.

I thrash, trying to wriggle out of his grasp or gain enough room to elbow him. "Stop it!"

"I've been nothing but nice to you, and this is how you treat me? *You?*" His voice is rising, arms constricting in anger. "Just how well do you know the commander? Are you letting him use this skinny body so you can get information out of him? Who are you, *really*?"

"Let go!" His hand squeezes painfully as he laughs at my struggles. I throw my head forward, then slam it backward into his nose. He releases me immediately, clutching his face and dropping to his knees. I can see blood dripping between his fingers.

He looks up at me with pure malice. "I should've known a pleb would whore herself out for a soft bed."

I can't help feeling an aching betrayal as his words sink into my brain, and I realize Springer was right about everything. I've let Drake use me for some unknown purpose, blinded by his handsome veil. As I look at him now, kneeling there pinching his nose to stop the flow of blood, I feel tremors of fear run through me. What have I done? Have I risked us all?

I finally manage to find my voice. "Think what you want, Drake. I can't make you believe anything different. But know this, we're done. I see what you are now." He shakes his head, and I turn and walk away.

After a few feet, his quiet words stop me in my tracks and root me to the floor. "Ah, Enora, it could've been good between us, but I see you've made your choice." I twist my head to look back at him. He slowly rises, wiping smears of blood on his arm, his eyes fixed on me. "No, we're not done. This is just the beginning."

I feel frozen, trapped in a nightmare as he saunters past. After a few minutes, I manage to unlock my muscles and run trembling hands across my face, trying to clear my head. My mind spirals through the incident over and over. Did I just inadvertently give him something so damning I could find myself in the crosshairs of some fatal accusation? I feel an urge to run, to save myself, but there's nowhere to hide. Not until Springer and I can leave in two days. Oh, God. So much can happen in two days. What is

Drake going to do with all of this? Am I going to be awakened in the dead of night, dragged out of bed by the rough hands of some Sentinel? Are they going to label me a traitor?

I don't know how long I stand there, but eventually, I shake off the fear and make my way to my room. Sinking onto the soft mattress, I let out a shaky breath and spend the next few minutes convincing myself that the most Drake could do is accuse me of sleeping around. How bad could that be? It's not like they have any proof. But inside, I know there is much more at risk. There's so much that must remain hidden.

In the end, Drake wasn't even after *me*. He used me to ferret out information that could lead to someone in power, whether from within the Company or without. In my carelessness, I led him to Bram.

CHAPTER FOUR

General Malvolia arrived at eight in the morning to tour the training facilities with a small contingent of specialized Sentinels. I'm sitting with my breakfast, a heaping plate of food I never seem to tire of when Springer drops that little nugget.

"She's here? In our unit?" I glance to the open door of the dining hall, imagining that a slew of Sentinels will charge through, and we'll be arrested. I haven't told him about my encounter with Drake.

"Don't look so panicked, Enora. It's just a routine visit."

We weren't on the grounds the last time she came here, having been on an assignment. I've never seen her in person, and, honestly, I don't want to. What if she knows? What if we're the real reason she's here?

The food I tucked into my cheek feels like a lump of tasteless mush. I grab my cup of water and wash it down, swallowing forcefully. It hurts my throat when it reluctantly slides into my stomach to sit there like an indigestible rock. I look at my plate, so full, and feel incredible guilt at the urge to throw the rest of my food away. Wasting food is a crime.

As I'm arguing with myself, Bram walks in, followed by a woman I've only seen in posters and Company broadcasts. She's not as tall as I imagined, but her demeanor is one of authority, and I note the way everyone stands at attention when she passes through the doorway. I get up awkwardly, fiddling with my napkin until Springer grabs it and drops it on the table.

Bram speaks clearly, his voice silencing all conversation in the room. "General, these individuals are the backbone of this unit, each highly trained and talented Sweepers and Pathfinders."

Her dark eyes sweep the room, cold and calculating. The black hair capping her head is tied back so severely that her face looks stretched from the constant pull. She looks thin, though not in the emaciated way of the rebels, but with a frame that is all hard lines and angles. There is no softness in her person. I have the urge to sigh in relief when her gaze passes over me with little interest. General Malvolia addresses none of us, only nods sharply once she's looked us over, and then turns toward Bram.

"Commander Williams, I would like to see the reports from recent assignments these ladies and gentlemen have completed. I'm sure their work will attest to the abilities you mentioned." Her voice is sharp and rather low, at odds with her narrow face and small frame.

"Of course, general. Right this way." Bram motions for her to precede him as they leave the room.

Perhaps it's just my inherent fear of the power she has, but I can't help feeling like her presence is a warning.

As Springer and I leave our headquarters on our next assignment, I breathe a sigh of relief. It always feels like a taste of freedom as we pass through the gates, and being away from the unnervingly watchful eyes of General Malvolia makes it even more pronounced. However, as we speed away in the Company, I wonder what the outcome may have been from her meeting with Bram. Was she impressed with the work of our unit? Did she put any undue focus on the assignments Springer and I have completed? Part of me wishes I could ask Bram, but the other part just wants to relish the freedom of leaving that place.

That's all I've ever really wanted. Freedom. It's what Bram and I used to dream about as we sat atop our hill, overlooking the sparse landscape of Prineville. Now, that seems like a lifetime ago. But I still want it. I wonder if Bram still dreams of it too.

Springer and I make our way through the barren world that surrounds every cluster of human habitation. As I look out my window, I begin to wonder how various rebel factions even survive out here. They must be forced to send out raiding parties constantly to keep, even their small population, from starving to death or dying of dehydration. A part of me wonders if it's worth it to go through all of that. The price of freedom is high.

I voice my question to Springer. "How do you think they manage it?"

"Manage what?"

"Living out here," I say with a sweep of my arm.

He slows the jeep, the electric whine of the engine dulling with the decreased speed, and waits until the vehicle behind us passes by before coming to a complete stop. "I don't know. They must have a stockpile of supplies or be raiding towns and facilities regularly."

There have only been a handful of vehicles on this road since we headed out, and they've all disappeared at this point, off to their own destinations. As a result, it feels even more desolate. I stare out the window as memories flicker in my head.

"I think about that night a lot."

He doesn't need to ask what I'm talking about. "I know."

"I wish I could go back and do it differently, you know?"

"Yeah."

Springer doesn't add anything. What is there to say, really? We can't go back and undo what's been done. If we could, there would be so many things I would change. So many people I would try to save, some of them from myself. We resume the trek along the empty roadway, quiet in our thoughts.

Our destination is a remote location. We've been directed here under the guise of investigating another infiltration of a food production plant. Of course, that facility is conveniently close to a division of the resistance. We've been tasked with scouting the area after the intelligence sector indicated a radius around the plant as a potential point of origin for recent raids. In reality, we are there to meet the commander of these rebel forces.

Unlike previous assignments, we brought all of our provisions and made camp to keep a low profile. It's hard to fully appreciate how many people were potentially involved in concocting this assignment. Individuals in multiple divisions must generate false information and pass it along to Bram through a chain of command. At any point, they could be found out. So much rests in our hands. It's a sobering thought.

Using Bram's coordinates, we drive to a midpoint between the food plant and the rebel bunker. It feels good to get out of the jeep and stretch my legs. The air is dry, as usual. In the distance, I see a few clouds and imagine them expanding, filling with water until they overflow, raining down on me. I can't help tilting my head back, pretending I can feel the water washing over my dry skin.

"What the hell are you doing over there, Enora? Falling asleep standing up?"

I flip him the bird and saunter toward him, reaching for the tent. "Ha ha."

It takes little time to set up camp. When we're finished, we just stand around for a few minutes, unused to having nothing specific to do. Our eyes find each other's and we both burst into laughter, so in tune that we can read one another's thoughts.

"It's kind of weird not having the DMC directing and monitoring our every move," I comment, thinking that this is the first time we've truly been away from Company surveillance.

"Well, we're not completely beyond their reach." Springer, the realist, points out.

I shake my head at him. "I'm not stupid enough to believe we're totally beyond their reach."

"You sure about that?"

"Shut up, you jerk!" I lunge at him, but he's fast and quickly escapes me.

Five minutes later, we're a bit winded and decide to enjoy our small liberation from the world. Springer hunts down two bottles of water and a couple of snacks for us to munch on. As I eat and take small sips, I think back to the rebels. I wonder how many people our little meal would feed.

SPRINGER AND I SIT IN A DIMLY LIT ROOM, TUCKED inside the depths of an old mine shaft, a rebel outpost with access to a couple of towns for small raids. It feels far removed from influence by the Company. Gone are the newly painted rooms and state-of-the-art technology. Instead, there are dank tunnels lined with concrete and metal reinforcements. Like so many others we passed on our way, this room is small and musty. Dust tickles my nose, and I wiggle it, wanting to rub my face but afraid my hands are covered with grime from our trek to this room. I'm also a little wary of doing anything that might inadvertently imply my distaste for the stink of this place. Like the previous rebel division we visited, there is a distinct smell of unwashed bodies and waste mixed with the staleness of dry earth and sour air. The scent seems to have filled my pores. I can't wait to get out of here and breathe fresh air.

I feel like we have been here for hours, though I know that it is just my impatience to leave rising to the surface. I begin to squirm in my seat, itching to get up. Springer surreptitiously reaches over and pinches my leg hard. It is all I can do to bite back a painful yelp. I settle for elbowing him and feel minutely better when he flinches. But, of course, this is ruined when I see him smirk.

It's almost surreal to think we will find ourselves in situations such as this many times in the future, ever since our initial contact. I try to avoid thinking about the assignment that led to that meeting. It inevitably forces me to recall the weight of a dead child in my arms.

That whole mission was just camouflage. I know that now--orchestrated by Bram to initiate contact with the resistance forces. It was never intended for everyone to be killed, which is one of those awful outcomes of manipulating a system designed to keep the truth hidden and maintain control.

Truth be told, Springer and I were too efficient and made our move before Bram had predicted before he could've reached out to the rebels and warned them of our presence. If he had, they would've been prepared, maybe they could've escaped back through the vents, and we would've simply been alerted to their attempt. There simply hadn't been time for all of the moving parts of the plan to align in a way that would've preserved human life. I wish I could go back in time and change it all, but wishes aren't real, and children don't come back from the dead.

I ruthlessly shut off my morbid flow of thought and shift my focus as the commander of the resistance walks into the room. I sit up straighter, determined to make a good first impression after everything that has been sacrificed to get me to this moment. From what Bram put me through to the choices I made without his interference, all I've done has brought me to this point. Springer and I are like two offerings that he can take or leave, depending on his impression of our commitment to further their cause.

The rebel commander is a very tall and broad hulking figure, though wiry as only someone who subsists on little can be. Although he is in his late forties or early fifties, he's by no means soft with age. He has the bearing of a man born and bred to lead troops into battle. I can't help comparing him to General Malvolia. While his size would dwarf hers, I think Malvolia would come out as the winner in a round of fisticuffs. There's something in her that makes her cunningly dangerous.

I see the commander's eyes swing to me and watch his slow perusal of my person. In his gaze, I can feel him take in my young, narrow face. I hardly look like the type who would be selected for the role of Pathfinder, much less someone who could help lead an opposition. Next to Springer's muscular form, I'm completely dwarfed, and I sense the commander's disapproval though he makes no overt indication of it.

He takes a few steps toward me and extends his hand. "Enora, it is a pleasure to meet you. I am Commander Guire. Bram speaks very highly of you and assures me of your ability to move our operations forward." His grip is tight, subtly crushing the fine bones in my hand until I feel sure they are about to break, and then he lets go and reaches for Springer.

"Your reputation precedes you, young man. Bram has informed me of your expertise in sniper-related missions, as well as your talent for getting in and out of some very challenging situations. I am happy to welcome you into our ranks. We can use someone truth your experience to help mold our soldiers into a force to be reckoned with."

"Thank you, sir. I have spent years honing my skills, but I assure you that I have not been successful on my own. My Pathfinder, Enora, has been instrumental in my ability to get in and out of numerous situations undetected."

Commander Guire's eyes fix on me as Springer says this, and I can see him weighing what he's being told. There is no mistaking the deference he has paid to Springer. On one level, I can understand this. He must have a large number of troops, and from what I've seen, many of them are young and inexperienced. Springer is a soldier who could hone their skills. Clearly, I will have to prove myself worthy of his praise. It's a bit irksome, but I don't let myself get riled.

Springer, ever mindful of the thoughts he seems to be able to read as they scroll across my brow, launches into the reason we are here and why the resistance needs us. "Enora and I risked detection to find information pertaining to the genetic mutations that are being created in Renascence."

Commander Guire interrupts. He turns to me and asks, "In this discovery, did you also learn the motivation for these mutations?"

Speaking in an even voice, I say, "Yes, commander. I found what looked like an evolutionary web, though not natural. Each offshoot of the web indicated an attempt to create a genetic modification. According to the information we found, you can even see these variations in the physical characteristics of the individuals, called the Aurora strain. We noted that these traits differ from those in the Sentinels of Renascence. The details on the civilian populace indicate that the Company is altering this mutation at a metabolic level."

The commander sits back in his chair, mulling over what I have just told him. "Bram indicated that you may have found crucial information for us, but I hadn't considered the potential nature of the intelligence."

Springer and I sit patiently while Commander Guire considers the information, no doubt thinking of ways in which to capitalize on it. Finally, he repositions himself and asks, "Would you consider an assignment to confirm what you have found? People must know about this. They deserve to know the truth. Are you willing to help us expose the Company by returning to Renascence?"

The answer to his question is as simple as it is terrifying. There is no doubt in my mind regarding the need for all of this to come to light, but I can't ignore the element of risk involved. For myself, I feel no hesitancy, but I acknowledge the ramifications to my parents, and this gives me pause. I hold tight to these feelings. If I don't, then I am truly lost. It is a razor's edge I walk upon. On one side are the arms of vengeance waiting to embrace me no matter the cost. On the other is my humanity, easily lost if I let black thoughts cloud my purpose. I must work on tempering myself and avoid straying too far over the brink.

"What information would you like us to attain?" Springer interjects.

I listen as the commander replies to Springer and outlines the information that would be most beneficial. It is up to us to decide which pieces we can access without posing too many risks. As the meeting concludes, the commander gives me one last assessment before leaving the room. It is a weighted perusal.

Rather than head back to our headquarters, Bram directs us to go directly to Renascence. He has taken the initiative by providing us with a directive to reassess the work we had done during our previous assignment, which will allow us to delve back into the darkness and anonymity that defines our false task. The operation he has us completing is to install updated surveillance equipment. I'm glad of the cover, as it will allow us to carry different types of gear that could otherwise be suspect. Being in a specialized division of the DMC also gives us a higher rank and deference from the Sentinels stationed in Renascence.

I have mixed feelings as we enter the heavily barricaded city of Brigford, a disguise to hide what is at its heart. While I welcome the chance to find the evidence we need to expose the Company, I also realize that the likelihood of accessing everything we've been tasked to find is slim. There was a bit of luck when I was able to slip in and out undetected during my last breach of the building. If fortune doesn't favor me in this venture, not only will the truth be hidden, but also my life and Springer's will be forfeit.

Having passed the security checkpoints, Springer and I make our way into Renascence. Nothing has changed, not in this place that rests safely in the womb of the city, only *I have*. I see the buildings and populace with new eyes and renewed purpose. As I consider the civilians, it is so obvious to me now. This 'designer breed' of human all looks the same, not in facial features but in stature and musculature. The chosen ones. The lucky ones. I have to curb my resentment as we park and enter the building where we are quartered.

Our room is on the same floor that we were housed in when quartered here before. This gives me comfort. I am familiar with the ins and outs of this part of the building, and we can more easily go unnoticed. Springer and I unload our gear in our respective bedrooms and then convene in the small sitting area. We begin talking quietly, making our plans.

"We should enter the tunnel system tomorrow. We must follow the same pattern of behavior that we did last time."

I nod in agreement. While I would like to jump right in, I understand the need to keep a low profile.

"Should I assume we begin at the same point as before?" he asks, and I can't help but appreciate his defer-ence to me. It gives me strength to feel his appreciation of my role in this.

I think his question over. "Yeah, that makes sense. I'd like to check on the equipment I placed there, and then we can make our way toward the city center."

Springer stretches, arms laced and reaching toward

the ceiling. I know he doesn't relish being in the dark again, but both of us are eager to be away from prying eyes. He stands slowly and reaches out his hand to me. "Come on."

"Where are we going? I thought we weren't starting until tomorrow."

"We aren't officially beginning our assignment until then, but that doesn't mean we can't get some fresh air."

He winks after saying this and hands me a small device that I will be using to collect photographic evidence of the population. It looks like a health monitor to anyone who may catch a glimpse of it, a common enough apparatus. The camera itself is specialized and provides measurement data and facial analysis information with each image. This will be used in conjunction with whatever documents we are able to get our hands on within the central headquarters of Renascence.

We make our way to the commons and find a shaded spot under an overhang. I do my best to stand up straight and look commanding, but I know it's a stretch. Springer folds his arms and pastes a bland expression on his face. He fits right in, of course. I hold the camera in my loose fist and begin taking pictures, turning my body by slow degrees so that I can capture both the individuals going about their day and the environment itself. The Sentinels of Renascence are positioned at various intervals, imposing figures whose grotesque mass makes Springer look petite. I catch a couple of them glancing our way, but their eyes scan our uniforms, and they leave us alone.

After a time, we stroll to another area and repeat the procedure. I see Springer look down at me from the corner of my eye, and I nod imperceptibly. This is my cue that I have what I need. We leave the area and head back to our room to look at the images I collected. I sit at the small table and link the camera to my computer. I use a back-door to do this to hide what I am doing from the Company, and I am careful to simply pull up the images and not upload anything into the system. The pictures are good, and with the additional information of height and mass the device overlays on each image, the similarities among the people are striking.

Having done all we can today, we pass the late after-noon and evening quietly, keeping to ourselves until the dinner hour during which we join the others who are quartered here. I let Springer do the talking, as usual. I have no interest in chitchat, and I'm not good at it anyway. I always find myself scrambling to think of what to say, and if I happen to hit upon a topic, it inevitably comes out sounding awkward. So I prefer to watch and listen.

The men and women who surround us seem so normal. They smile and laugh, just like anyone. But I find their presence such a contradiction. Don't they under-stand where they are and whom they're protecting? Don't they have an inkling of what this means to the people outside of this tiny community? How can they not see the wrong in it? I want to ask these questions, but I keep silent.

As I settle in that night, I review in my head the structure of the tunnels and various locations that I had mapped. We will be tampering with a few of these to allow for future access for the resistance. Next, I visualize the locations that had shown some sign of a breach and decide I will avoid these, as they are now known to the Company and would be more easily detected. From there, I begin to narrow down potential areas, and when I have decided upon some possibilities, I burrow my head into my pillow and quiet my mind. It begins tomorrow, and I must be ready.

CHAPTER FIVE

The pipelines under the micro-city of Renascence welcome us like an old friend, dark and inviting, telling us we are safe, that our secrets will be kept hidden. I can see the ever-present tension in Springer's shoulders ease as we head deeper into the subterranean system. We light our way with flashlights and head to our original starting point.

As before, Springer keeps watch as I investigate the device I had placed here months ago and check for any tampering. From my inspection, it looks as though no one has touched it, and I feel relieved that our work has potentially gone undisturbed. I prefer to remain in a bubble of obscurity and hope that I find most, if not all, of our mechanisms in similar condition.

The hours pass slowly as we make our way through the labyrinth of tunnels. We are both impatient to put in the time to establish a routine and therefore become less noticeable to anyone who may be monitoring our movements. I realize this will take a few days, and I find it hard to tamp down my desire to get things moving and break into central headquarters to find the information we need. Springer is better at hiding his feelings, but I can sense his anxiety and try to distract us by inviting some conversation to pass the time.

Questions have been growing in mind over the last few weeks, and being in this place, with no one watching and listening, is the perfect opportunity to voice them and get some answers. "How was it that Bram rose to such a high-ranking position so quickly?"

Springer chuckles. "I've often wondered the same thing. As I told you before, he clearly had help from others on the inside. But I've always thought there must be someone in a fairly high position orchestrating it all. It can't just be underlying types who somehow organize all of this. The only thing is, what branch of the Company would this person be in? And how did they even find out about him?"

"He's really smart." I grimace a little as I say this, thinking of my own rather mediocre performance in school. "In fact, he had a strong feeling his academic aptitude would probably get him recruited. However, he didn't want that life. At least, I thought he didn't. Now, I'm not so sure."

Springer doesn't press me on that path of thinking.

"Whatever he may or may not have known, to get recruited, someone must have known who he was and been following him over the years as he got closer to graduation. I've assumed it must be a family member of some kind or perhaps an older acquaintance. There must have been someone, and once he was in the system, he moved up quickly."

I stop mid-stride, an unpleasant thought worming its way into my head. "I don't want to know what he did to get where he is now."

"Come on, Enora, you know him well enough that he played his part, just like you, and got where he is because someone moved him there like a game piece on a board. I mean, you can't seriously think he moved up the ladder on his own?"

Clearly, the answer to that question is, yes, I can, and I had. I feel stupid having assumed that to become the commander of my unit, Bram must have done something so admirable by the Company's standards that he was advanced quickly with no reason for suspicion. That admirable action, in my mind, has always been laced with carnage.

"If that's true, then who helped him?"

"As I said, I don't know who. He never told me, and I never asked." Springer admits. "You have to realize that there are many of us working from the inside and probably at every level. There's no other way we'd be here. You and I just happen to be the only people, to my knowledge, that has discovered that DMC control has extended to genetic modification. It's an idea that has been floated across differing groups, but not in the sense of what we found here. I think most of the implications were of genetic traits being selected to build up populations of Sentinels and such."

It's like the drones that I grew up being suspicious of. It makes sense that what I observed and felt was spot on, and that others would have noticed the same physical traits. So many machinations, so many people working behind the scenes. It makes me proud to be a part of it and sad for the costs.

"I should have known he wasn't just trying to turn me into a drone, and I feel bad that I thought the worst of him. But now, I still wonder why it had to be this way, you know? Why did Bram think this was the only path?" I shake my head, feeling guilt over the killings I've been a part of settle in my stomach like some lump of indigestible food.

Springer reaches over and runs his hand slowly down my back in a comforting gesture. "Bram knew how you would react, Enora. He knew you'd think the worst of him, but it didn't matter if you never understood the truth behind his actions. It was worth it to him to get you out and give you the tools you'd need to see the Company for what it really is."

"Yeah, I get that. But I've killed, Springer. I'm a killer now." What I leave unspoken is how Bram had always been the better of the two of us. He's the one who always looked out for me when we were kids. To have him thrust me into this violent world and knowingly mold me into this is hard to accept, even now. And yet, Bram is the one who always saw the big picture. The goal must have been clear and the acts of violence, an inevitable outcome for him.

"The things you've done don't define who you are, Enora."

"Yes, they do. Words are empty. It's actions that have the most meaning." I stare at the ground, thinking about the things I've done.

"Okay. I see your point," he admits. "But let's look at what you're doing now. Being here, switching sides, and fighting for the liberation of everyone, is an act that will affect the lives of thousands. Don't you think that's part of who are too?"

"I guess."

"What is Bram's motivation? Why do any of this?"

"Because he wants me to be free," I say quietly, turning toward Springer.

"Yeah. He wants us all to be."

"He was my best friend, you know."

"He still is, Enora."

I look away into the blackness of another tunnel and think about how true that is. I have so much I would like to say to Bram, both good and bad. But I can't. I have a job to do. Bram is counting on me. So many people are, I suppose, and I won't disappoint him. I pick up my gear from where I dropped it and continue on, Springer walking quietly next to me.

We spend some time establishing a noticeable routine and then begin planning the infiltration of the central building of Renascence. I will primarily be using my camera in our first go-around. This will enable us to minimize the time we are in the building, thereby decreasing our risk of discovery. If we are successful and do not alert anyone to our actions, then we can attempt another breach and get more specific information that I will scan onto a data drive.

When it's time, I use my equipment to hack into the security system and review the various recorded scans as individuals enter and exit the lowest, and most heavily restricted, level. The system files show that the remote monitoring systems are scheduled to commence during a 12 am – 5 am window. I am relieved by this, as I rationalize that this would have been changed had the Company been alerted to my prior intrusion.

Once I have established a way to hack into the security system and make a video feed loop to overlay any remote security monitoring, I pack up my gear and meet up with Springer, who has been waiting at a junction.

"All set. Nothing has changed since last time, so I don't think we'll have any trouble getting in and out."

"Good. I just want to get this done and get us out of here without incident."

I couldn't agree more. It puts me on edge to be working in a location such as this. It is a heavily guarded compound, and should we be discovered, we would simply disappear.

After returning to our quarters for dinner and sleep, we're too anxious to get any rest, waiting for darkness to come and the hours to pass. At two in the morning, I override parts of the security system that monitor the building of our sleeping quarters and the route we take to get to the tunnels. I feed video loops into the program that I had created the night before so that we can exit the building without notice. Once done, Springer and I leave quickly and head underground.

I sense his nervous energy as he waits for me to put everything into place before we break into the basement level of the headquarters. I try to block out his restless strides as I work, but it's distracting, and I find myself unable to concentrate fully.

"What the hell, Springer? Your pacing is driving me nuts," I whisper into the dimness.

He stops immediately and looks at me, a disgruntled expression crossing his face. "Sorry."

I pause and look more thoroughly at him. "Are you okay? This isn't like you."

He looks away and sighs. "I don't know. It just doesn't feel right. I can't explain it."

I lift my hands off of the keys I've been stroking as I burrow my way into the building's security. "Do you think we should go back?"

I see him weigh my question, and I wait while he works through countless scenarios before responding. "No."

"Are you sure? Did you have some premonition or something that we're going to get caught?"

"It's not this that's bothering me," he says as he waves his hand in my general direction. "I can't explain it. It's just a feeling like something is in play that I'm not privy to."

I sit back on my heels and wait for him to go on. He's the stalwart one, and I'm the hothead. So for him to be worried about something has me spooked. "Have you heard something from Bram while we've been here?"

I can see the moment that I have hit upon some truth, and his decision to hide it from me, flash across Springer's face. But I'm having none of that. "Don't you start hiding shit from me!"

He huffs, no doubt irritated that I can see his deception. "I haven't heard from Bram."

I know that statement is too generic when it comes out of his mouth. "I will assume that you should have heard from him. Is that right?"

"Yes, that's correct. I have been in contact with him

daily since we left for Brigford. He should have contacted me yesterday, but I have heard nothing."

"So, what does that mean?"

"I don't know what it means, or even if it means anything. It just has me on edge, that's all."

I think over what he's said and left unsaid. If Bram is in some way compromised, then we are also at risk. I squelch my natural reaction to flee and decide we need to continue and get what we can, while we can. I feel like a clock is ticking, and we are going to run out of time if we sit here and debate our actions.

"Let's get this done."

Springer straightens his shoulders and joins me as I input a few more commands and indicate that it's time to enter the building. Our familiarity with the layout lends itself to efficiency. We head to the room with a map showing an intricate web of genetic modifications that have been whittled down to one dominant strand, the Aurora strain. It's the characteristics of this mutation that the Company has deemed most desirable and worthy of furthering. I take multiple images as Springer hangs back, having never seen this evidence of God-like arrogance. I understand his shock, though I have already shared the information with him. It is different to see it staring you in the face.

I am eager to get our work done quickly and hustle him out the door and into the file room. I take pictures of the room itself to give the impression of the multitude of files, while Springer pulls out some examples for me to document. I steel myself against the horror of seeing the frozen images of tiny, deformed faces and focus instead on the data I can capture within each file, especially the time-stamps as they are damning. Then, when I have what I need, I face the inevitability of entering the last room we plan to photograph.

It has been quiet since we entered the building, no inhuman noises have radiated through the emptiness, but I still feel like I can hear them, like the ghosts of those cries are echoing inside my head. I stand outside the door to what can only be described as the maternity ward, such an innocuous term for something so vile. Springer gently brushes against my shoulder and then holds out his hand, silently indicating that I can remain behind and he will take the pictures we need. I shake my head. I will do this.

I slowly turn the knob, and we enter the room, immediately assailed by the smell of disinfectant and human misery. I scan the space and the rows of beds, each occupied by a being that hardly qualifies as a woman. They are nothing more than mutilated wombs housed in inhuman shells.

As I look at their bloated bodies, I have to wonder which generation of the Aurora strain these women fall under. Their gross deformities, from their filmy eyes to their misshapen limbs, indicate they are part of this whole process. But which part? Do they carry one of the traits the Company is breeding? Are they somehow passing these qualities along to future generations? I walk up to the first bed and take photos of everything before moving on to the next. People need to see this. They need to understand.

I don't mean to bump the bed when it happens. I was simply leaning over too far. But the unavoidable jostling stirs its occupant to some awareness of my presence. I find myself looking into eyes covered in a milky film that cloud any true sight. The mouth slowly opens, a maw of blunted teeth and drool. I feel my heart start to race as a low sound erupts from that gaping hole. I want to cover my ears, but my arms feel anchored to my sides, and all I can do is stand there and look at this prisoner strapped to the bed, this swollen corpse because she can't be considered any kind of living thing, this is not living. As I pause there, frozen by the guttural moan emanating from this being, her distended belly begins to undulate under the thin covering of a blanket. I am helpless to stop my eyes from tracking the slow movements of the mutation growing in the womb of this poor vessel.

My eyes widen as I see the muscles of her abdomen seize in a spasm. The moan becomes a hoarse grunting as though the tightening is causing pain. Still, I stand there rooted to the floor, completely oblivious, as an alarm begins to beep softly from a machine monitoring her physical state.

Springer grabs me by the arm and pulls me from the room. He shakes me to full awareness before rushing me out of the building as quickly as possible. I am fully recovered from my shock by the time we enter our access point and grab my computer to reestablish the remote monitoring and security systems.

Springer leans against the wall in relief after I look up and indicate that everything is back online, and says, "That was too close."

CHAPTER SIX

By the next afternoon, we have still not heard from Bram. Springer and I decide that we need to get out. While leaving prematurely carries its risks, we are reluctant to stay within the walls of this city if something has gone wrong and our cover is blown. We pack our gear and make our way to our vehicle. I am filled with tension as we head to the first checkpoint.

Springer chats casually with the guard as our documentation is verified. I am in awe of his ability the blather on while I sit there, a ball of nerves that probably couldn't even utter a coherent sentence. It seems to take longer than normal to see the gate open and be waved on, but we soon find ourselves beyond the perimeter of Renascence and heading through the decrepit streets of Brigford. The difference in these two communities is striking as we leave the opulence and enter a run-down city littered with broken buildings and starving people. I try not to look too closely as the jeep passes through streets of misery. Instead, I channel my energy into solidifying my purpose.

I know I won't be able to take a full breath until we pass through the gates of Brigford, and I focus on this, willing us to move faster. As we are heading to the last checkpoint, the final boundary standing between freedom and capture, Springer receives a message from Commander Guire. It is simple, to the point.

You are compromised.
Exit the city now.

Springer grabs my hand and squeezes as we pull up to the last barrier. I can see the pulse racing in his neck as spots of perspiration bead across his upper lip and forehead. I've never seen him scared, and his reaction increases my anxiety.

So softly I almost miss it, he mumbles, "I promised him I'd keep her safe."

He hands over our documentation to the guard. The casual banter is gone. I watch as the guard leans over to look into the jeep, verifying its occupants, and I turn my head to look directly at him, determined to do more than just sit here. Pulling myself together, I stare the Sentinel down for a few seconds before he leans back out of the window and glances once more at our paperwork.

Finally finding my voice, I say, "Our commander is expecting our report promptly, and I'm sure he won't appreciate hearing about any delays in our return." I arch an eyebrow, daring the guard to respond, and am rewarded by a tight swallow followed by a short wave to move on. Springer's hand moves away from the gun he had been pulling from the holster on his hip. I hear the soft click of a safety clasp as he secures it. We travel for a few silent minutes before Springer lets out a gush of air and turns to me.

"Damn, Enora, you saved our butts back there. All I kept thinking was how many people I'd be able to take down before they got to you."

His comment surprises me. "Springer, you can't risk everything just for me."

"That's why I'm here, Enora. It's why Bram paired us. He knew I could take care of you."

"You have taken care of me. But I'm not some helpless thing, you know."

He laughs. "Obviously! The way you talked to that Sentinel was pretty badass."

I shake my head. "I can't believe I said something that actually made sense."

"You never cease to surprise me." He gives a tight smile as the jeep speeds down the road.

"Where are we going?"

I watch him mull this over. "Well, I think it's safe to say the only place we can go is to the resistance."

It is a hard reality to face. This situation means more than not returning to our DMC headquarters. I wonder what happened and what this will mean to our efforts and Bram and my parents. I face the reality that I will probably never see any of them again. I feel queasy as I consider what the Company could do to my mom and dad. Will they take my parents away, like they did Safa? Will Sentinels drag them from their nice home and throw them to the ground, smashing their faces to the pavement in vengeful glee? I lean forward slightly, hugging my waist.

"You okay?" Springer asks. I shake my head. "You feel sick? Should I pull over?"

"I'm not gonna throw up." I rock a little as ugly scenarios dance in my head.

"Enora?"

"My parents. They'll get my parents."

Springer is silent. All I hear is the electric whir of the engine and the sound of other vehicles passing us in a whoosh of air. I knew this would happen. There was no other outcome. This is what I was truly sacrificing by turning traitor. I knew it when I made my choice, but I chose this despite that hard reality. And now, I will have to live with the consequences of my actions. More blood on my hands. Will they ever be clean again?

"This must be why I haven't heard from Bram." Springer finally says.

"Do you really think he's been compromised, or is he just reducing a risk to us by not contacting you?"

I am so hopeful that it's not as bad as I fear, that maybe my parents are okay, that maybe Bram got them out.

"I'm not sure. It would make sense for him to take precautions, but I've had this feeling that something wasn't right, and now it seems to be confirmed."

"Is there any way to save them?"

Springer just shakes his head. I look out the window, not seeing the barren landscape, as my eyes are cloudy with unshed tears. Unfortunately, I already know the outcome of this situation.

A FEW HOURS LATER, WE ARRIVE AT THE RESISTANCE base. We are expected. Our young guide takes us to a small room and asks us to wait. Springer sits in one of the hard chairs, and I pace the floor. The movement keeps my mind busy and prevents me from imagining what could be playing out in some other room to the people I love.

We have been waiting for twenty minutes when Commander Guire enters and pulls out a chair. He indicates that I should sit. I'm tempted to stand instead, unable to face sitting and hearing things I dread to know but relent, as I don't want to make a scene in my current frame of mind. As soon as I have seated myself, a woman enters with a small device that looks like a scanner of some kind. Her hair is lank and stringy, tied back in a bun. It makes me wonder how long it's been since she washed it. Like everyone else here, the bones in her face are too prominent, and she's painfully thin. With hard eyes, she looks us over.

Commander Guire indicates the woman and says, "This is our resident software expert, Lee Hayes." The woman nods but doesn't smile. "She will be scrambling the chips in your wrist. Once she does this, your location will be untraceable in any system, even ours. It is important for you to understand that while this will permanently affect the chip, we cannot actually remove the device. There is a failsafe feature in it that sends out a signal if its hardline into your body is severed, as it would be in the case of removal."

"But haven't they tracked us to this point already?"

"They've tried, but a team working from the inside has been able to hack into that system to interrupt the signal. That team is also responsible for the communication we got to you and your ability to exit the city. Interrupting the traces by the DMC was a temporary solution until we could get you both here. Of course, our contacts also took the liberty of removing as many personnel files as possible to shield you from identification by various surveillance systems, but our backdoor into their network was discovered before we could access much. Rest assured, the DMC knows who you are and will be trying to find you."

I take all of this information in as Lee approaches with her equipment. I twist my arm to expose my inner wrist and wait as she presses the device against me. I hear her push a couple of buttons, and then it's done, and she moves on to Springer. I rub the area, feeling the small, raised bump, and wish I could just rip it out and be rid of it.

The unfriendly woman leaves the room, shutting the door behind her, and I watch the commander fold his hands and look pointedly at us. It is time to hear what happened. I scoot close to Springer, drawing some measure of comfort from his proximity. Commander Guire clears his throat and launches into a rendering of what he learned.

"For some time, the Company has been casually monitoring Bram." He begins.

"Why? Had he done something suspicious?" I know my voice is defensive, but I can't help the feeling.

Commander Guire looks directly at me when he responds. "What I can tell you is that Commander Williams' rapid ascension to his current position was an anomaly that put him on their radar early on. You must realize there have been others within the Company who used their positions to become informants." He pauses, and I nod, acknowledging that there have probably been many rogues over countless years. "It is customary for individuals who are quickly moved up in rank to be tracked. The majority of these people have nothing to hide and are removed from observation after a few months."

"In the case of Commander Williams, their scrutiny rekindled after you were recruited." I feel a pang of guilt when he says this. I can't help feeling that, if not for me, he would never have been at risk.

"The fact that you and the commander came from the same town did not go unnoticed," he continues. "To more closely watch your movements and any potential connection to Commander Williams, or another individual in power, an informant was enlisted to get close to you and gather information. Do you know of any such individual?"

I look down, unable to meet his eyes and see any glare of accusation. "Yes, sir. I believe I know who that is." Of course, I know who. Drake. I let him in and let down my guard. I was blind and careless.

Commander Guire's voice is understanding when he says, "Ms. Byrnes. These people are very good at what they do. They have been trained to get past any reservations you may have and gain your trust. Unfortunately, you're not the first person to be a victim of it, and you won't be the last."

I squeeze my hands to keep my self-control and look him in the face. Springer warned me that I shouldn't trust anyone, but I didn't listen. If only I had. I take a deep breath and let it out slowly. "Thank you for that, Commander Guire. But I do hold myself responsible. I should have known better."

He accepts what I say without comment. "This informant..."

"Drake." I interrupt. He looks at me questioningly. "His name is Drake, the one who was sent to spy on me."

"Very well. Drake reported to an intelligence branch of the Company whose sole purpose is to ferret out anyone trying to infiltrate the DMC. All information gathered within this sector is shared with the head of the division, General Malvolia. She has full authority to act on any intelligence she receives."

My heart sinks as I hear her name, a name that I've heard all my life. General Malvolia has earned a reputation for ruthlessness. Her voice and face accompany everything from posters touting loyalty to broadcasts of traitorous consequences. She demands allegiance and exacts this expectation with harsh repercussions to any who refuse to give it.

Commander Guire's voice interrupts my thoughts. "Apparently, Drake passed along suspicions of your loyalty to the general's branch but had not made a strong connection to Commander Williams' role until recently." I feel the weight of guilt constrict my chest. "The informant's information led to a deeper analysis of the commander's actions from the point of his own recruitment to yours. Of particular notice was any promotion of you after commencing training. From what they put together, it became clear there was unusual interest in you, and when you were placed in his unit within a short time, these suspicions, in conjunction with Drake's report, were confirmed."

I think about this and wonder why Bram pushed me so

hard and so fast. It seems as though he must have known that his time was running out.

Commander Guire leans back in his chair, watching emotions flit across my face before going on. "When Commander Williams was alerted by an insider from another division of the Company that he was under increased scrutiny, he began to falsify documentation to shield you and Springer from discovery. He specifically fabricated information relating to your assignment in Renascence. In the end, he did everything in his power to lead all potential threats directly back to him, thereby implying that he was acting alone. General Malvolia was provided a full report and made the decision to interrogate the commander to determine who else was part of this infiltration."

Commander Guire doesn't detail the interrogation, but I have a vivid imagination. There is no mercy for traitors. A spectacle has to be made to remind anyone thinking they could betray the DMC. I look into his face and see him deliberating in his mind what he should or should not tell me. But I need to hear it. "Please go on."

I can see a reluctant glimmer of respect in his eyes. "The general herself traveled to the training compound to witness the event. Commander Williams was dragged into a yard, his legs unable to support his weight, having been broken at some point. Guards strapped his body to a pole while a full audience looked on and listened to a list of transgressions, some true and others not. A Sweeper stood at the opposite end, and upon General Malvolia's order, fired a bullet into his brain."

The room begins to spin as his voice continues. Was it Drake who pulled the trigger? I feel like I'm going to black out and blink rapidly, trying to focus on his voice.

"Following the execution, General Malvolia ordered a full investigation into Commander Williams' unit, with particular emphasis on you and Springer. At this point, an alert had gone out to me from one of our operatives on the inside. An immediate message was sent to Springer along with increased efforts to block all tracking of your locators to ensure your safe return."

It takes a moment for me to realize that Commander Guire has finished speaking.

I am numb.

"I assume the Company is suspicious of what we may have seen in Renascence?" Springer asks, breaking the silence.

Commander Guire glances at me and then looks directly at Springer. "They know that you and Enora are connected to Commander Williams. You are slated for interrogation, but the extent of what they suspect you may have found has not been shared with me. From what I have learned, the commander had been prepared for this inevitability and taken pains to minimize the suspicion that you may have seen anything of interest to the resistance when in Renascence. As you know, reports were falsified. Your altered assignment was not related to the subterranean system. Whether or not these fabrications have been discovered has not been made available to me."

I squeeze my eyes closed as I take it all in. But, of course, he protected me. He has always protected me. When I open my eyes, I look at the commander and ask, "Did he give you any kind of message to pass along?"

"Yes. He said you would ask." Commander Guire nods to himself and relays Bram's last communication. "Commander Williams asked me to tell you to remember the hill and the dreams you made there."

I take that in and stand up, unable to sit with this knowledge roiling in my mind, and walk over to a mesh-covered window that looks out into the corridor. He's gone. That's all that I can think. He's gone, and I will never get to tell him that I understand what it's all for now. I will never have the chance to thank him for leading me to the truth, for helping me get out of a community in which I would have become some nameless, faceless nobody. I will never get to tell him that he was always more than my friend in my heart.

I can't focus on what Springer says to the commander but hear the man stand and leave. The door shuts quietly behind him. Springer walks to where I am, struggling to maintain my fragile control. His hands gently rest on my shoulders, and my body begins to quake. I manage to remain standing for a few more seconds before my knees give out, and I collapse into his arms, muffled sobs ripping from my throat in grief so deep that I feel I will never be free of it.

LATER THAT NIGHT, I AM ALONE IN A SMALL COT while thoughts tumble through my brain. I thought I knew it all. I was so sure of my convictions, those blinding things that hid the duplicitous nature of the one person I should have known best. And now it's too late. I must live with the choices I made along this ruthless path that was set out before me by secretive hands. Bram's actions led me to a life riddled with guilt for the things that I've done, but they also brought me to the truth.

Although I was not there to witness, my mind paints pictures of the events that I cannot shy away from visceral, bloody scenes of torture and execution. The movie in my head spins a story of brutal hands dragging a strong body from his bed. Unforgiving light blaring into a face I hold in my heart while a mind bitterly defends itself against a barrage of verbal attacks meant to uncover a truth it has kept hidden for so long.

Did that assault last long?

Was he suffering while interrogators tried to batter down his defenses?

Did he welcome the gentle hand of death when it reached for him?

To these questions, I will never have an answer. The

only truth I know is that a bullet entered his brain, and now he's gone.

I ache thinking of him and all he did under a guise I was unwilling to look beyond. To finally be able to stand back and see it all for what it truly was, all of his machinations designed to lead me to a reality I never knew existed. He was my most faithful ally and greatest friend. Perhaps he was even more than that. Maybe his love for me transcended friendship to such a degree that he was willing to risk his life to protect mine and show me the way. Whatever his motivations, I am left with bittersweet memories.

I want to beg forgiveness for the hateful anguish I directed at him, although I know he would tell me to let it go. He knew me so well. All that is left is to muster my strength and continue, as he has asked me to do. I owe him that much.

Truth be told, I owe Bram so much more.

OVER THE NEXT THREE DAYS I FIND THAT I CAN forget when I am put to work, my mind is occupied when my hands are busy. I've been asked to look over the broad range of devices the rebels have stored but never used due to having no one with the right training. Some of the items are newer, but most are old and in sore need of updating, having been stolen over many years during various raids. As I sift through the mess, I have my doubts that I'll be able to get even half of them running.

It's quiet work, which is probably best. I'm not good company most of the time, overwhelmed with sadness for Bram or a ball of worry for my parents. Trying to maintain a conversation with anyone here is beyond me, not that anyone seeks me out to begin with. I find that my work doesn't last enough hours, and when it ends, thoughts I have kept at bay, pummel my brain.

Have my parents been taken from their home? Are they sharing the same fate as Bram, or are they being shown mercy? Does mercy even exist for relatives of traitors? These are the questions that have no answers until the DMC chooses to provide them. It is hard to live day to day with such awful uncertainty.

Springer leaves me alone much of the time, having been requisitioned to begin training the men and women who make up the military force. He's got his work cut out for him with that motley group. So many of them are young, the more seasoned individuals being part of the groups that go on supply raids. I see the lines of frustration at the reality of this place when he returns to our quarters after a long day.

Mealtime is the hardest part of living down here. Springer and I join the others in what barely passes as a dining hall. The tables and chairs have all seen better days, and the food is barely edible, which makes me thankful for the small portions I have to choke down until my stomach is gnawing with hunger. Since I was recruited, I've enjoyed a life of luxury, relatively free to eat or drink whenever I feel the need. Now, hunger and thirst are constant companions. It's hard to believe I was even better off growing up than I am now. That time seems so long ago.

But I can take the scarcity. The looks we get during each meal are the hardest part. The majority of the people we encounter are more hostile than friendly. I know this is, in part, due to those we killed during the raid, but there's more to it than those losses. Many times I have caught eyes glaring at me as I eat my ration, looks that zero in on the food passing to my mouth. I feel the weight of those looks.

I try to keep my focus, determined to somehow make Bram's death worth it. I need to know that all of this means something. But I feel like I know only part of the story. What did he die for? The rebels? The truth? *Me?* I'm just some kid struggling to make sense of a world that's gone crazy. As the hours and days tick by, I feel like I'm losing my edge, like the anger that has kept me determined is being chipped away under the weight of my guilt and grief, and worry. How can what I'm doing be important enough to lose my family? Why did he choose *me?*

I will never know Bram's true motivations. Just as I will never know what memories flashed through his mind in those final moments and if any of those thoughts were of me. I hope they were. I hope his mind took him back to the hill we used to share. To the times we spent huddled under the stars, dreaming of a better life.

They were good dreams.

CHAPTER SEVEN

Springer pulls me from my job of helping a group of young teens learn how to use my refurbished scope and mapping system and brings me to our quarters. Then, closing the door, he pushes me gently onto my cot.

"What are you doing?"

"I need to show you something, Enora. It's from Bram."

I gasp. "B...Bram? How?"

"He must have hidden it in my pack before we left that last time. Somehow, he must have known that...that his time was short." He hands me a thumb drive. I look at him in confusion.

"It's a video file."

My eyes widen as I look at this tiny piece of Bram in

my palm. Springer hands me my computer. "I already downloaded it. You just need to push play."

I can't stop my hands from shaking as I press the key to start the video. Before I'm ready, Bram's face fills the screen.

"Hello, Enora."

My eyes fill with tears at the sound of his voice, and I sob once.

"I'm sorry I can't be there with you to see this through. But I know you will continue the fight for the truth. I've always known you could do this."

His image looks down as he lets out a soft sigh. "I'm sorry that I've put you through so much. I know you must hate me, on some level at least, and I can't blame you for that. This fight we're in, this power we're trying to expose, is the true purpose. Unfortunately, there's a high cost to see the DMC for what it really is. I wish things could've been different. But if wishes were real, I'd be with you now.

You need to know that there is still something worth fighting for. Enora, do you remember those dreams we shared when we were young? Remember how we used to talk about a world where water ran free? Well, I've found it. Up north. There's a huge reservoir just outside the border. It's in the outlands and will be a rigorous journey, but you can get there. You and Springer need to share the coordinates I'm giving you with the resistance. They don't know any of this and can help you form a scouting party to find it.

You'll never believe this, but it even rains there, something about the wind currents and mountain range surrounding the reservoir. That body of water is constantly replenished and could sustain millions of people, and the Company is hiding it. They are lying to everyone to protect that resource. I'm not sure why, but you have to find it and show the people. They need to know that it exists. They deserve to know what's been hidden from them. The future doesn't need to belong to these mutations they're creating. The truth is, there is enough for all of us!

Enora, I'm giving you the last thing that I can. Hope. I know you'll find a way to get there. You can do this. Do it for me. Do it for the dream we had together. I love you."

Tears are streaming down my face unchecked when the screen goes black.

Springer doesn't say anything. He just sits next to me with his arm around my shoulder. It takes a while for the anguish to leave, but when it does, I feel resolved.

Commander Guire is in the control room when Springer and I walk in, along with Murdock and a woman I have never seen before. Like the two men, she is dressed in clothing that is a step up from the rest of the people living down here. Her brown hair is cut short, giving her rather square face, a somewhat masculine look. Like many others I've seen, her pale skin is pocked but beyond these shallow scars is an open expression that could've been attractive and inviting if we lived in a different world. Introductions are brief.

"Enora, this Sergeant Susan Quinn. I have been awaiting her arrival before we go over the intelligence that you and Springer brought to us. Her division is in a prime location for supply raids, and she'll be instrumental to our future plans. Let's look at the data now that we are all here so that we can discuss how to use this information."

"Yes, sir. But before we begin, I wanted to let you know that Springer and I found a hidden communication from Commander Williams. It was just discovered and could be powerful evidence, along with the data we'll show you, to bring the Company down."

Three pairs of eyes look at me with genuine surprise. Commander Guire sits forward. "Commander Williams sent you a communication before his death?"

Springer replies before I can. "He hid a flash drive in my pack. On it is a video file that you all need to see."

The commander indicates the screen in the front of the room, and Springer moves toward it. Like everything else here, the machine is old and takes a couple of minutes to warm up. Once it does, Springer loads the file and presses play. Again, a grainy image of Bram fills the screen. I'm ready for it this time and suppress the pang of grief I feel as he begins talking. Everyone watches silently, so stoic that I cannot read their reactions. When the video is complete, Springer pulls up a map with coordinates.

"As you can see," he begins. "The reservoir Bram discussed is just over this mountain range, about fifteen hundred miles from here. If we take a small contingent of your soldiers, we can get there within three days."

Springer's idea is met with silence. I look over their faces and am surprised to see Commander Guire smirking.

Before I can ask what he finds so funny, he says, "It's been a while since I've heard the story of the hidden lake."

"Excuse me?" I ask, feeling a flare of righteous anger on behalf of Bram.

"The idea of this place has been around for many years. I'm not sure how many, to be honest. What I can tell you is that it's a myth. There is no lake that the DMC has kept hidden."

A feeling of disbelief falls over me. They don't believe Bram? Do they think it's some kind of fairy tale?

It's hard to keep my voice even and calm. "Commander, how can you be sure it doesn't exist? Has anyone gone out there to find it?"

"Enora, there simply is no such thing. If there were, it would've been found long before now."

"But how can you be sure? The Company has control over *everything,* especially information. Don't you think they'd keep this from coming out? If people knew there was a place like this..." I can't go on when I see their various expressions of pity and annoyance.

Commander Guire looks hard at me. "It's a story, nothing more. There is no body of water tucked away in some place that rains. This is one thing DMC isn't hiding.

I'm sorry. I know how much you both want to believe this, but it's just not true."

I feel deflated and fall into the back of my chair, the cold plastic sinking into my bones. They don't believe Bram. It's hard to understand how this information can just be brushed off as some fanciful story, but apparently, that's all it is to them. Could Bram have been mistaken? I think about how excited and sincere he was and can't believe that he'd fall for some crazy tale about a place that didn't really exist. He has the coordinates. He was so sure. I don't bother saying any more on the topic but, inside, I can't let the idea go. If there is a place like this, someday Springer and I need to get there. For Bram.

"You both need to focus on the evidence you've found. It's this information that is real and actionable." Commander Guire's eyes hold mine for a few seconds before he continues. "Now, let's move on to what you uncovered in Renascence."

And just like, Bram's message is dismissed.

Murdock goes to the computer and pulls up files of the images I took of Renascence. I set aside my irritation and focus on the frames in front of me. This is tangible, I tell myself. I've seen these things in person, and like the water Bram spoke of, my discovery of the Aurora strain is powerful and will further the rebel cause. People need to understand this too.

I walk to the screen. "Where would you like me to begin?"

Commander Guire looks at the various file folders. "I would like you to take us through the events as you experienced them."

I walk to the wall screen and point to the file containing the photos from our first day. Then, as pictures of the commons, and the various Sentinels stationed there, fill the screen, I begin to explain what Springer and I noticed during our time in Renascence.

"You'll note the physical similarities in the Sentinels. Unlike the guards seen outside of Renascence, these men have much more pronounced musculature. We believe that there are two mutations within this city, the Sentinels you see, being one of them."

I wait as our audience begins to confer, often highlighting what they are saying by using the images on the screen. I continue to let them talk and then open the next bundle of images of the civilian population. As soon as the pictures flood the screen, all conversation stops.

"These are the civilians of Renascence. You can see the extreme differences between the two mutations. This populace has a smaller, more compact body, and we assume that this is a by-product of the mutation itself. As for its purpose, I am not a scientist. However, we do know that the mutation is rooted on a metabolic level, as indicated in data I found. Unfortunately, we were never able to get too close to these individuals, as that would've raised suspicion. As you will note, they all appear to be very young, which ties into the other data we found."

The images show the physical traits in stark relief, as each individual's picture is overlaid with measurement data, including mass and height. I move to where Springer sits and listen halfheartedly to the conversation going on around us. After a few minutes, Commander Guire indicates that I continue, so I pull up the next file.

"This is the evolution of the Aurora strain. As you can see from the photo, numerous offshoots either didn't exhibit the desired traits, resulted in some other failure, and were terminated. This one branch has been the focus of continued research and propagation. When looking at the general population, you can see a markedly high percentage of individuals under the age of twenty. This seems to indicate that the experimentation has been honed to this particular strain for a rather short amount of time. I think this will become more clear when I pull up the next set of images."

I open the data from the file room and display the photos of the babies, their deformities illuminating the screen.

"My God," I hear Sergeant Quinn gasp.

They gather closer to the screen, pointing at and discussing various pieces of information from the files displayed. I hear them comment on the dates of various files, creating a skeletal timeline of when the efforts had been started. This predictably leads to the scrutiny of the timestamps. The men make the same connection that I had before turning to me and asking for clarification.

"Do these timestamps refer to birth and death?" Sergeant Quinn asks.

"Yes, ma'am. We believe something must have gone wrong, either physically evident or otherwise, and they were terminated immediately. Springer and I happened upon a mass grave under this building that corroborates our theory."

There is a brief discussion before Murdock speaks up. "You mentioned the population seems very young. If that's the case, who are the parents?"

I pull up the last bank of images, cringing slightly when I open a file containing the blank stare of one of the women.

There is a collective gasp when the picture bleeds onto the screen. I can see a level of distaste in the face of each of them, but I also note something more. If the general population of the U. S. was shown this information, there could be an uproar and potential rise against the DMC. I can't help thinking that knowing about a hidden water source would add even more impetus to fight, but I have to smother that thought. I seat myself next to Springer and watch the group continue their discussion.

Finally, Commander Guire turns to us. "You have provided us with information that is as shocking as it is essential. The people need to be made aware of this. Your efforts have become the greatest piece of evidence we have in our possession. Enora, you have proven to be everything that Bram had implied, and I am grateful for your efforts."

I take his outstretched hand and return a firm shake, pleased that I have proven myself while also mournful at the reminder of the cost.

"We would like to discuss this matter further and will inform you of our decision on how to proceed." He tells us.

After that, we are dismissed.

As we walk the corridor back to our rooms, I force myself to relive the moments that enabled me to capture the images we have shared. This is the strength Bram would want me to draw from. As I consider the potential ramifications of moving forward, Drake's face pops into my head, adding fuel to my emotions and allowing me to smother my grief and worry.

I turn to Springer. "I want him to take him down."

"Who?" Springer asks.

"Drake!"

"I don't understand. Where did *that* idea come from?"

"He's the reason we're here, in this stinking hole in the ground! If not for Drake, Bram wouldn't be dead."

"Enora, I understand your anger, but you have to realize that Drake's just a pawn. Nothing he did was on his own. In fact, I bet General Malvolia is behind all of his actions. After all, he was part of the intelligence community, and she runs that division. Nothing goes on that she doesn't approve first."

"What if he's the one who pulled the trigger?"

"You don't know that."

I look away and stare at the faded cement wall covered in peeling paint and grime. I want to lash out at someone. It's easier to direct my anger at Drake. But the rational side of me understands what Springer is saying. There's no way Drake did anything without the direction of a superior. But she's untouchable, protected in her authority. I could get to Drake. I huff, resentful that I can't just target my anger at the one person who wormed his way into my life and then ripped it apart.

"This is not about Bram," Springer says quietly.

"I know. I just want...I don't know what I want."

"Yes, you do. You want the world to know the truth."

WE FIND OUT THE NEXT DAY THAT SHOWING THE world what we have uncovered is not the directive we've been given. Instead, it has been decided that the images and other data we collected only tell part of the story and could be construed as digitally manipulated fakes. We need tangible proof to add more credibility to what we have found.

"You want us to do *what*?"

I'm thankful that Springer has voiced the question because I have been left speechless. I was so sure that we would never be asked to return to Renascence, that the risks we took and the data we found were substantial enough to reveal the ugly face of the DMC to the world.

To be told to go back is beyond imagining. It seems more reasonable to follow Bram's suggestion to discover the body of water the DMC has hidden for countless years than to go back into that place.

"We are asking that you and Enora utilize one of the access points you installed and obtain one of the civilians. A child is most sensible. They would be easier to remove from the premises and keep subdued." Commander Guire says pragmatically.

"You can't be serious!"

"I assure you that I am, Springer." I hear the censor and warning in the Commander's rebuke and want to warn Springer not to push it.

"I apologize, Commander," Springer replies, but I can hear the incredulous edge in his voice. "But you have to know that there is little chance that Enora and I will be able to complete this mission. I would like to suggest that we put our efforts into finding the water source Commander Williams informed us of. I believe that discovery would be a catalyst for our efforts."

"We are not wasting time and resources to chase a fairy tale, soldier. Now, I agree that the risks of returning to Renascence are great, but it is a chance we need to take for the greater good. This is your assignment."

When Springer doesn't reply, Commander Guire continues. "Sergeant Quinn's division is located approximately twenty miles outside of Brigford. It is to that division that you will be transported." I glance at Sergeant

Quinn, who's been standing silently in the corner while the Commander is speaking. She nods in acknowledgment but adds nothing.

Commander Guire's voice continues to outline what amounts to a suicide mission. "The sergeant's people have already been informed of your assignment, and plans are underway to support the infiltration of the subterranean systems both leading into and under the city. Enora, you will be provided with numerous schematics to determine the best route. Additionally, you will be provided with all the necessary equipment to enable you to enter the access points you created in your last assignment without alerting anyone who may be monitoring the tunnel system. As for the asset, we will give you drugs that will knock out your acquisition to minimize any physical confrontations in transport. Once you have returned to her division, the resident doctor will begin an analysis to fully understand what we're dealing with. Once we have enough information, then we will determine the best course of action to inform the public."

The directive is so callous in its matter-of-fact presentation, and I am left wondering if I really know with whom we have joined forces. The child he is asking us to steal is a mutation, but it's also a living thing. I am uncomfortable by the commander's utter lack of feeling. I don't bother voicing any hint of refusal or challenge, though. I know that it is pointless to say anything. We are being given an assignment, and, in the end, is it any worse than the murder we have done before?

Springer and I walk slowly back to our rooms to prepare. There is a hopeless feeling in the way our shoulders slump. Closing the door to our only haven, I lie facedown on the cot, unwilling to fully accept the task before us. Stealing one of the mutations? Just getting into Renascence is going to be challenging enough but kidnapping a kid is beyond imagining.

"Why can't we just leave and go look for that lake Bram told us about?"

"Enora, I can't understand a thing you just said," Springer snaps as he shoves gear in his pack.

I roll onto my side. "Why can't we just look for the lake? We'd have a better shot at living through that."

"People like us don't get choices."

"Well, maybe that needs to change!" I snap.

"I agree. You gonna change it?"

"Maybe."

Springer shoves my legs over and plops down next to me. "What if we can do both?"

I make a face, and he holds up his hand before I can start arguing. "Just hear me out. If we do this, get a kid and prove to everyone what the Company is doing, then maybe Commander Guire will let us search for the lake. Think about it. No one else can do what we can by breaking into Renascence, which gives us some leverage. Let's show them how essential we are and use that."

"Okay," I mumble, but my heart isn't in it. This task seems risky, and I wonder if we're expendable pawns in someone else's game.

I get up slowly and start packing my own things. A photo slips out as I'm stuffing an extra set of clothes into my bag. It's one I've kept with me since leaving Prineville but have looked at only a handful of times since I left. The image is of my family from a couple of years ago. The Company took yearly pictures of us to keep in their database, and we always got one to keep. My dad had given me this one before I left as a new recruit. I trace the faces of my parents. None of us is truly smiling. It's not that kind of picture. There was no spontaneous laughter or joy at the moment.

My fingers stroke the edge of the image. "What do you think the Company is going to do to my parents when they find out we've stolen one of the mutations?" I have to think of my future actions and hold onto the hope that they have been untouched up to now. It's easier to go on if I imagine them safe back home.

Springer stops what he's doing and looks over at me. I can feel the weight of his stare but keep my eyes on the images of my parents. "I don't know."

"Yes, you do."

"You can't help them now, Enora."

"I know, but that doesn't make this any easier. You're lucky you have no one to worry about."

"That's not true. I have you."

How easy it is
To look upon an aberration
And see only the ugliness
That spawned its creation
To imagine the stain of deceit
Marring its perfect skin
Like a nightmarish brand
It is harder the see the reflection
Staring back at you from innocent eyes
Showing you the evidence
Of your inhumanity

CHAPTER EIGHT

Our arrival in Sergeant Quinn's division is met with some fanfare. It seems that many of the residents of this small faction have been told details of our assignment as we are greeted enthusiastically. It's such a different reception from before that I'm taken off-guard until I realize that we've done nothing to this group of people to warrant any hostility. None of their friends and family was killed. To these people, I am not a monster.

Though the reception is better, the conditions certainly aren't. Only so many warm smiles can mask the gaunt features, and nothing can erase the smell that is already invading my nasal passages with an acrid stink. As we make our way through the underground system, it's clear the place is a little newer than Murdock's division. While it's still musty and dim, the walls and various metal structures look less worn, but those differences are too few to make it seem even remotely pleasant.

Sergeant Quinn is expecting us when we arrive in her office. "Springer. Enora. Welcome to my division. I know you want to get started so let's go over specifics."

She begins with a brief review of the system of tunnels that we can infiltrate to make our way to one of the access points below Renascence. I am already familiar with the schematics, having requested detailed maps prior to our departure. In my head, I have selected the most opportunistic point of entry and combined this information with my prior knowledge of the micro-city itself.

Gaining access to a child of the most pliable age is the bigger issue. I have talked to Springer at length about this, and we both agree that an older child will put up more of a fight, and one too young could be too difficult to manage. So we have decided on the area of the city that houses the five-to-six-year-olds. It is more centrally located, and we are more familiar with that portion of the system, giving us an advantage for making our way into the compound and also getting out undetected.

"Do you have any questions at this time?" Sergeant Quinn asks.

Springer speaks up. "What is the contingency plan if things go wrong?"

"There is no contingency plan," she says matter-of-factly.

"I see."

"You both need to appreciate the risks to each person in this division if we tried to save you, should something happen. Not only could I lose a good portion of my troops, but I would also be exposing my entire division. That is not something I can risk."

Resentment bubbles to the surface when she says this. "Are you saying we're expendable?"

She looks at me in silence for a few seconds. "In war, we are all expendable." I open my mouth to argue, but she stops me. "How can I put your lives above those who have lived within these walls since birth? Are you so much better than they are? More valuable? More important to the cause? I understand what I'm asking of you both. Do you understand the desperate situation we are in?"

I look down and breathe deeply. The scent of misery washes through my nose. "Yes."

"You and Springer have skills and experience that far surpasses anyone living down here. This makes you valuable weapons. As the head of this division, I will use everything at my disposal to benefit my people and our efforts. But I will not place your lives above those of the individuals who have bled and suffered in this place."

Lifting my head, I look her fully in the face. "We will do everything we can."

"I know you will, and I appreciate the risks involved. It is my sincere hope that you complete this task and return to us safely."

Springer speaks up. "Thank you, sergeant. We have every intention of making it back."

We leave the briefing shortly after and are taken to our quarters by a man who is probably under thirty but looks at least ten years older.

"I'm Hal," he says, holding out a hand for us to shake. I can't help noticing the grime in every crease of his fingers and palm as I take it. He has an open face, devoid of guile. Like everyone we've met, the skin under his thatch of dirty blond hair is sallow and stretched across the bones of his face. He's taller than me but a few inches shorter than Springer. His thin frame makes him look small compared to Springer's muscular form.

"I'm Enora. This is Springer." I watch as he shakes Springer's hand. I like his honest face.

"You're both Company people?"

I look at him and feel only a polite curiosity. "Yes. We were a team. Sweeper and Pathfinder, before all of this."

"It must be very hard for you, being here, I mean."

I assume he means this whole place, the smell, the lack of food, the lack of hygiene. "It's an adjustment, but I wasn't an elite. Neither was Springer."

"I mean leaving your family."

Being reminded of them is a punch in the gut. "Yes."

"I know what it's like to lose people you care about."

I expect him to say more, but he doesn't, and I don't press. It's only a couple of minutes later that we arrive at our room.

"Here you are."

Springer steps inside first, setting his pack on a cot. He turns toward Hal, holding out his strong hand. "Thank you, Hal."

Hal bobs his head and walks back down the dimly lit tunnel.

The room is a little larger than our previous one, though the cots are the same hard things with springs poking into the thin mattresses.

I feel tired just thinking about what we're about to do. I sit down on the lumpy hardness. "Are we ready for this?"

"Yes," Springer says with a certainty that surprises me. "There isn't anything we could do to prepare ourselves any more than we already are."

"I guess you're right. It just feels like we're not going to walk away from it, you know?"

"Would you rather leave and go off on our own?"

I think that over for a moment. "No. I'm not ready to do that yet."

"Then, we're ready for this. You know the ins and outs of Renascence. So do I."

"True."

"Commander Guire needs us to succeed, Enora. So do the people here. In fact, everyone does. They just don't realize it yet. But what we're going to do is help to light the fire, you know? Just imagine how you and your parents would've reacted if you found out that the DMC was creating a breed of human that would replace all of us. Do you think you would've just blown it off?"

He's got a good point. If the Company hasn't taken my parents already, they'll see what it is I'm trying to do when the rebels show the world the evidence. "No, something like that would've opened our eyes long ago. That's what it'll do now, if they see it, if they're still free."

"I think they are. You need to believe that they are."

I know what Springer's telling me. If I picture them safe in their home, it's easier to accept the risks we're facing. I want them to see and understand why I became a traitor. "Thank you, Springer."

He winks at me, and we turn our attention to preparations. As I pack, I let my mind wander to my life before any of this. Since I was young, I have been taught at home and at school, that the DMC is here to help. The DMC will provide for us. The DMC will protect us.

Now, they will not be able to protect themselves from me.

We enter the tunnels at night at a point well outside the border of Brigford, hoping that the lateness of the hour will provide some measure of concealment. The distance we travel to reach the access point is considerable and provides us with an unwanted amount of time to fully consider what we are about to do. I don't share my worries with Springer and note his quietness as an indication of his reluctance to share his thoughts. It is only after we pass beyond the perimeter of Brigford that I break the silence.

"Thank you, Springer."

"For what?"

"For believing in me when I didn't. I can't imagine coming this far with anyone else."

I can see that my words have surprised him. It is unlike me to share my feelings without any prompting, and I know what I've told him has an impact.

Springer looks at me with soft eyes. "When Bram first told me about you, I thought he was biased. While I knew you must have had qualities worthy of merit, I felt your former relationship likely skewed the lens he saw you through."

Springer pauses, letting what he said sink in. There will always be a twinge of sadness when I think of Bram and how we used to be. And there will always be regret for so many things left unsaid. But it fills me with a sense of peace to hear that Bram spoke so highly of me and strongly believed in my ability to face such significant challenges. I have never seen myself as someone with inherent strength and fortitude. Bram saw it. So, therefore, it must be.

"He was right, you know, about all of it. It didn't take long for me to see that."

I smile, though it feels strained. "Bram must have seen the same traits in you. He was always a good judge of character."

"Yeah, I guess he did."

"If we don't..." I pause, trying to find the right words. "If I don't get a chance to tell you, I want you to know that it was worth it. And if things go wrong, I want you to get yourself out. You need to promise me that you'll get out."

I punctuate my request by grabbing a fistful of his shirt and pulling him toward me. "*Promise me.*"

"I will, Enora. I promise."

There is so much left unspoken, but it is there all the same. Springer is my only friend. He's all that remains. My parents, I will never see them again, at least that's how it feels. The moment passes, and we turn toward Renascence.

Entering the passages under Renascence is accomplished fairly quickly. On our last assignment, Springer made the access points easy to manipulate for anyone who had knowledge of their whereabouts and mechanics. Once on the inside, we make our way to the central hub of this micro-city to orient ourselves and then infiltrate the correct housing unit. The tension we feel as we get closer to our target is palpable. If things don't go as planned, the results will be catastrophic for one or both of us. This thought is prevalent in my mind as we move stealthily through the darkness.

Once we arrive at our destination, I pull up an image of the structures above the surface. The five-to-six-year-old housing unit is close to central headquarters but still far enough that our entry point will not be observable from any video surveillance. We move through an offshoot of the tunnels and position ourselves below the housing unit. Springer passes me, visually scanning our surroundings, ready to act on any threat of discovery. As he completes his reconnaissance, I pull out my equipment and prepare to use my infrared scanner to see if anyone is moving about on different levels of our target. My perusal doesn't show anyone making rounds, so I move to the security system and deactivate the necessary components so that he can enter the building unnoticed. Springer returns by the time I have finished.

"It's time," I say, and he looks at me, into me. It's not goodbye.

Springer and I decided to revert to our traditional roles of Pathfinder and Sweeper. I will keep tabs on the security systems and heat signatures while relaying what I see to Springer using my equipment. As usual, his role is more precarious than mine as he will be acting as a Sweeper in a much different capacity than before. Instead of eliminating the target he reaches, he will be acquiring it. In addition, to increase our chance of success, Springer will release gas into each level he enters, thereby rendering anyone awake unconscious. On the surface, the plan sounds foolproof. But I worry that we have missed something and may find ourselves trapped.

I watch Springer's figure, illuminated in glowing red on my screen, enter the building. From my display, I can see the forms of sleeping children in two rooms that adjoin a separate space where I note another individual sleeping. I infer that this is an adult in a supervisory role and relay the information to Springer as he moves toward the first sleeping quarters. Once outside the door, I watch him pause as he reaches into his pack and pulls something out. When I see him crack open the door and push it into the room, I know he releases the gas.

As Springer waits a designated number of minutes outside the door, I quickly scan the remainder of the floor and then check on the status of the remote security feed. I let out a breath when I see that his infiltration has not been noticed, and my overrides of the system remain intact. I move my scope back to his location in time to see him enter the room and scan the occupants. I know that he is looking for a small, easily carried and controlled child. I watch as his form moves through the beds and then stops at the end of one of them. Instead of watching the actual kidnapping, a task I am still uneasy with, I go back to check all systems and the building itself.

When I switch back to Springer, he leaves the room with a bundle strapped to his back, a small, innocent form glowing faintly on my screen. My heart rate increases as he makes his way down the hall and to the entry point, pausing to check his surroundings before exiting the building and heading toward me. I wait in my position until he is well within the pipelines and then recheck the housing unit for any movement before switching the remote security system back on.

We've done it. I let my shoulders droop in relief. We have incontrovertible proof of what the Company has kept hidden with this act. The world will look at this mutation, which will spark an uprising.

I smile in grim satisfaction.

CHAPTER NINE

The boy, this alien thing, doesn't wake as we begin to travel away from Renascence. He is small and utterly oblivious to our theft. From a mere foot away, he looks so normal, human. When I get closer, I can see what was not visible as we observed the Renascence population before. His skin has an odd texture and appearance. As I lean in, shining the light on his arm, I see strange webbing all over the surface. It's faint but so unlike my own arm's appearance. There are no pores visible, just slight discolorations creating a strange pattern on his skin. I reach out and run my finger along it, thinking it'll be raised, like a scar. But it's completely flat. When I pull my hand away, I rub my fingers together. They are covered with some form of residue. I reach out again and touch his arm. There is a film covering his skin like a waxy secretion.

"Did you feel his skin?" I whisper to Springer.

"Yeah. Weird, isn't it?"

"I wonder why it's like that?"

"Me too." Springer cranes his neck a little to look at the boy's arm. "Hey, let's get moving. I don't like being here."

I agree, and we move quickly in the darkness, feeling a sense of relief with each step.

As we walk, I feel a need to suppress a weight of guilt that threatens to seep into me. Why should I feel guilty? The end justifies the means. At least, I think it does. In my heart, I'm not so sure, and this disquiet puts me on edge.

How exactly will they use this child?

What will happen to him once the world sees him, combined with the information I gathered?

Is he expendable like so many others seem to be?

These are the thoughts that spin through my head as we travel deeper into the passageways, farther from the point of turning back. Springer is wrestling with his own misgivings when he stops and turns to me. "Did we do the right thing?"

"I don't know."

I watch him crane his neck to look back and assume he's considering the ramifications. "It doesn't feel right."

"Should it feel right, Springer? I mean, even though we need to do this, to show the world, it's still a human being. Sort of."

He puts his hands on his sides and drops his head, thinking about what I've said and how to proceed. The child on his back, wrapped in a cocoon of unconscious-ness until now, begins to stir. I see his eyes flutter before they focus on my face. They are a startling color, almost golden, and they are penetrating against the sheen of his light skin and blond hair. My voice lodges in my throat as I see him look at his surroundings, trying to under-stand where he is and who we are. His awareness makes me cringe inside, like something slimy. Fear begins to crawl across his features, and I worry he will start screaming.

A callous part of me, one that I shy away from facing, considers gagging him to keep him quiet. I shake off the thought and say, "It's okay. We're not going to hurt you."

His face crumples as his inherent recognition of danger fully sinks into his brain. I am unprepared for his small voice.

"I don't like it here."

A tearless sob accompanies this statement as he begins to squirm, trying to free himself of the backpack that Springer placed him in. His legs swing, hitting the back of Springer's thighs, while he works his arms free and tries to lift his body upward. Springer hasn't moved, seeming para-lyzed by the child's struggles.

I move closer and begin roughly patting the boy's back, not entirely sure how to comfort him and irritated at having to. "It's okay."

"I want to go back," he cries, continuing to fight his way free.

"Hey," I say softly, trying to temper my voice. "What's your name?"

He looks at me, lip quivering. "Ander."

"That's a nice name. I'm Enora, and this is Springer. Ander, would you like to go on a little adventure?"

"No. I want to go back."

"We can't take you back."

The boy looks at me, pleading. "Why?"

I'm at a loss to think of what lies to tell. Finally, Springer speaks up. "There are lots of people who want to meet you. They are very excited to see you."

Ander looks at Springer's profile as he says this and then back at me, as though needing confirmation that it's the truth.

I nod, adding with fake enthusiasm. "Yeah, there are lots of people who have heard all about you."

How can I stand here lying to this little kid? The fib tastes like dirt in my mouth. Have we made an irrevocable mistake? I shake my head, arguing with myself. No. This had to be done. The truth must be told. It's finished, and there is no way that I can retrieve it or change its course.

Thankfully, Ander swallows my lie and stops struggling. "Can I go back after I meet them?"

"Sure you can."

But in reality, I doubt that he will ever be returned. It would be too risky to try to sneak him back in. Instead, I foresee him becoming an example for the resistance to such a degree that his image could be plastered across the nation in an effort to further their cause. After all, what could other tests reveal if his skin and eyes look so different? Inside, he may be unlike anything anyone could've imagined. If that's the case, why would they send him back into the arms of the monstrosity that created him?

Children must be inherently gullible because he innocently accepts what Springer and I have told him as truth. I'm relieved by his acceptance and eager to get moving. I hand him a gadget from my pack to play with to keep him occupied. He seems enthralled with it. When he eventually asks if he can keep it, I tell him yes. I see a smile spread across his face. This seems to be the tipping point between fear of us and blind acceptance.

As we resume our trek through the tunnels, Ander settles back against Springer, fiddling with his new toy and utterly at ease in the presence of strangers. I often feel his eyes drift to mine, and I sense that he sees me as some guardian in this strange situation. I'm uncomfortable in that role. I consider what he may have known of his parents. If the woman who gave birth to him was one of those monstrosities, he doesn't really have any family. He was grown in a lab. To me, he's a means to an end. I can't let myself be tied to him and potentially use him against me. I harden myself.

Minutes pass in silence as we continue onward. The quiet gives me time to consider the potential outcomes of Ander being shown across the country and potentially the world. I assume that technology gurus, like Lee, will be able to hack into the broadcasting systems around the nation to spread the word to millions.

When this happens, will there be a revolution? Will people truly see this as an unveiling of the DMC? Or have they become so defeated by the harshness of life that this won't faze them at all? What if his mutation, along with evidence of a hidden water source, were made public? Would both of those secrets be the Company's undoing? There are so many unknowns, and I don't like being left with loose ends, not knowing how my part in this will affect so many lives.

Ander's voice breaks my reverie. "Do you think Miss Martha will be worried about me?"

Crap. Maybe he has a mother after all. "Who's Miss Martha?"

"She takes care of me. And she takes care of the other kids too. She's nice. Miss Martha gives me candy some-times." I'm relieved when he explains. This lady must be a specialized caretaker for the kids in her facility. I don't know how I'd feel if he had an actual mother, and I am thankful I don't need to explore that possibility.

"Does she live with you and the other kids?"

"Yeah. But she has her own room. I'm not supposed to go in her room, but I can if I have a bad dream."

Listening to his small voice is like shining a spotlight on how incredibly young he is. I've rarely been around little kids, and it's hard to know what to say. He's some strange being that I can't relate to. I look at Springer and jerk my head, indicating he should say something because I'm at a loss. He gives me a look and shrugs his shoulders, obviously unsure of what to say himself. I glare at him.

His brow creases, and then he asks, "So what kind of candy is your favorite?"

I roll my eyes. Candy? Really? That's the best you could do? But I see Ander's head tilt as he considers the question. Honestly, I'm kind of curious about his answer myself since I never got to eat candy as a child. Water credits didn't allow for such frivolities.

"I like the hard kind. I can suck on 'em for a long time. Miss Martha says I gotta have my candy cause it makes me strong."

That's weird, I think to myself. I wonder if what he's been given is a flavored supplement of some sort.

Springer keeps up the conversation as though completely at ease. "Oh, what flavor do you like best?"

"I like lemon best. But sometimes the top of my mouth gets sore if I suck on it too long."

It's easy to imagine his mouth puckered around a sour lemon candy.

I hear Springer's short laugh. "You're very lucky that Miss Martha gives you candy. Enora and I didn't get candy when we were your age."

"Why not? Were you bad?"

Anger is laced in my voice as I reply, "No, I was a good kid, but candy isn't free, and we didn't have enough credits to buy it."

"What's credits?"

Figures. Of course, he doesn't know what credits are. He doesn't even have a tracer in his wrist. None of them do in that place. It irks me to think of it, and my reply ends up coming out too curt. "Most people have to work and pay for the things they eat."

His nose wrinkles as he takes this in. "That's too bad that you didn't get candy. If I had some, I would let you have a lick."

The sweetness of his offer gets under my skin despite my irritation. I force myself to admit that he's just a little boy, ignorant of the world, and I have seen too much of it.

We pass the remainder of our journey through the darkness with small talk. Springer grows more comfortable as time goes by, and soon I can see him relax. Ander eventually asks if he can get out and walk, having grown tired of being strapped on Springer's back. We stop, and I lift him out. He stomps his feet a few times and tells me he needs to wake them up. Then he takes me by complete surprise by grabbing onto my hand as we resume walking. I try to pull my hand away, but his hold is strong, and I don't want him to start crying if I force him to let go.

He has a tiny hand, completely engulfed in mine, another testament to his innocence, another black mark against me, and the resistance. I reluctantly hold it, aware of his trusting fingers lacing through mine. I look forward to reaching the jeep and heading back to the rebel bunker just to be able to put some space between him and me.

As we walk, I think about what our actions mean for our future. Ander is now our responsibility, much as I hate to admit it. Without us, he would be safely tucked in his bed. It is a heavy burden when I really consider what this means, but there is still a part of me that is human. The Company and my own thirst for revenge haven't smothered it completely.

CHAPTER TEN

A small cluster of people is waiting for us when we drive up in the beat-up jeep. Most of them look at Ander with natural curiosity, but I can't help notice the disdain stamped across a couple of the faces.

Ander squeezes next to me, looking for safety in my presence, though I've done little to engender such an action.

I cringe as Ander's voice pipes up while pinching his nose as we head inside. "It smells yucky in here."

Reaching over, I roughly pull his hand away from his face, but his comment hasn't gone unnoticed. Taking a glance around, I see flashes of annoyance and resentment on the faces of those within earshot.

"Sh," I hiss as we head into the dimness.

I assume we're going directly to Sergeant Quinn's

office, and I'm surprised when we end up in the medical quarters instead, though I suppose I shouldn't be. Obviously, they will want to look Ander over, and that is the most appropriate space.

Sergeant Quinn is awaiting us as we enter the room. She looks Ander over from head to toe, noting the features I had described so precisely and then zeroing in on the markings covering his skin. Her mouth curves in a satisfied smile at the end of the perusal. "Enora. Springer. It's good to welcome you back. And who is this?"

I pull Ander away from my side and force him in front of me so that Sergeant Quinn can get a better look. It's hard to resist wiping the waxy film that's left on my hand onto my pants. "His name is Ander." I feel Ander's body push against the hand I have pressed to his back, but I keep him steady as he is assessed by calculating eyes.

"Excellent!" Sergeant Quinn gives us congratulatory pats on the arm. "I will admit that I wasn't entirely confident you would be able to pull this off. I'm very glad to see my assumption proved wrong."

"Springer is the one who took the most risks." I drop my arm and Ander quickly darts back to my side as I say this. I take a small step away, but he follows me like a shadow.

"Yes. I am sure you both took risks." Sergeant Quinn is positively gleeful as she claps her hands together and explains the housing arrangement. "Now, as you both know, this facility is approaching capacity, and space is limited. In light of this and your roles in the next part of this operation, I have decided that Ander will share larger quarters with the two of you. In this way, you will be able to keep him under your supervision, and this proximity may prove beneficial as we move forward."

I barely manage to keep my jaw from dropping. So I have to share a room with Ander and Springer? It's like some twisted family unit, only the kid is a mutant, and the 'parents' are some strange couple who kill and kidnap people for a living. I feel my head shaking and see the sergeant's eyebrows elevate in surprise.

"Is there a problem, Enora?"

Damn. Why can't I keep my cool and remain stoic like Springer? Instead, I lamely say, "I don't know anything about kids, ma'am."

She chuckles. "He's not a real kid, Enora." When I don't react to her comment, she explains her position further. "Look, the two of you are an integral part of our operations, and there may be times when you will be taking the child to various locations to keep him out of the hands of the DMC. When that happens, he needs to be with people he's grown accustomed to. It reduces the chance for unpleasant incidents."

Springer, quiet until now, speaks up. "Am I to understand the boy is solely our responsibility?"

The sergeant turns to him. "That is correct."

Springer nods, and that's the end of any further debate. I bite my tongue and swallow the protests itching to come out. I look down at Ander, still tucked against my side. He looks so normal, but it's just an illusion. I guess that's what really gets to me. Looking at him is a reminder of the world I thought I knew, that façade hiding an ugly truth.

Sergeant Quinn's voice redirects my attention as she introduces us to the resident doctor, a woman with a gaunt face and bulging eyes. "Doctor Eva Kane will be completing a thorough assessment of the child. We can use the data she collects as further proof of the creation of a mutated race."

Dr. Kane looks at Ander with a decidedly clinical expression, as though the child is some kind of bug she wants to stick with a pin and put under a microscope. Ander cringes away from the doctor as Kane moves toward the boy, pasting a smile on her face that is more creepy than comforting, and crouches down so that she is at eye-level with Ander.

"Hi, I'm Doctor Kane."

Instead of replying, Ander turns his face into my side. The doctor looks up at me with accusation, as though I have some control over how the child reacts. I raise an eyebrow in challenge, daring her to say what she's implying. I watch as her eyes grow cold and feel that I have inadvertently crossed some boundary. Springer senses my mood and intervenes before I do or say anything that could result in unpleasant repercussions.

"What is it that you need from the child, doctor?

Perhaps we can help as he feels more comfortable with us."

Kane's eyes move to Springer, losing some of their iciness. "I need some samples so that I can do a comparative analysis to verify your findings."

"And exactly what does that mean?"

"I'd like skin, blood, and urine to start with. After I've examined that, I may need other samples."

Springer nods and lowers himself to his knees so that he can look Ander in the face. "The doctor wants to make sure you're a healthy boy. Can you be brave and help him?"

Ander turns his head to look at him, eyes wide in fear but too naive to know what this 'help' really entails. The child looks from Springer to me, and I reluctantly smile in encouragement.

This seems to be all the boy needs as he shyly says, "I can be brave."

Springer gives him a big smile and then hoists his little body onto the cot, which serves as the examination table so that the doctor can begin. Thankfully, Dr. Kane has enough sense to begin with the easiest task first and takes a small scraping of skin and secretions from Ander's arm. This doesn't seem to cause him any pain, and he gives me a big smile, proud of being so brave.

I can't help but play my part and say, "That wasn't so bad, was it?"

"Am I all done?" He then looks at Dr. Kane and asks, "Are you going to give me candy like Miss Martha?"

"I don't have any candy. The people who live here don't get sweet things like that."

I don't miss the condescending tone in Kane's reply, but Ander is oblivious to it. "I like candy."

"I'm sure you do," she says with little feeling. "Now hold still while I take some blood."

Having come out unscathed by the skin sampling, Ander shows no fear when Dr. Kane brings out a needle. However, it becomes apparent that the good doctor has had little practice drawing blood from children. She sticks the needle in three times before she can find a vein, and in the end, I am forced to sit on the cot and wrap my arms around Ander to hold him still. When it's over, the child is crying tearlessly against my chest, whimpering about how his arm hurts and he doesn't like the doctor. I don't blame him, but I keep my mouth shut.

I let Springer take charge of the last test, peeing in a cup not being something I can handle. While I'm waiting for the two of them to return from the bathroom, I watch Kane place samples onto slides and look under the microscope. Ander looks like a pretty ordinary kid until you get close or touch his skin. But I'm most curious about what's on the inside, and I can only assume that more advanced equipment will be needed to see all of those variations.

Dr. Kane scribbles notes on a pad of paper as I watch her work. I am impatient to leave. Her clinical attitude is unnerving, and I sense a loathing of Ander, which I assume, could translate into something more menacing. While I may not like being responsible for the kid, I can't deny my accountability in this, and a proprietary feeling creeps into my head. Finally, Springer returns, and I stand up, eager to go. But his face stops me.

"What?" I ask him and watch as he lifts the small cup with Ander's pee in it. It takes me a moment to realize what I'm looking at. Instead of a cup of yellowish liquid, there is a layer of a thick, almost milky substance. I'm about to blurt something out when Springer shakes his head, indicating Ander's watchful eyes.

I quickly rearrange my thoughts and say, "I guess you didn't really have to go, huh?"

Ander looks at me oddly. "Yeah, I did. But only ever go a little."

"Oh." I can't think of anything else to say and watch as Kane gingerly takes the cup, tilting it this way and that to see the slow movement of the viscous mass. Ander looks confused by all the fuss, but his attention drifts, and I see him yawn.

"Fascinating," Dr. Kane remarks, looking at Ander with speculation. "You can leave the boy here. I'd like to run a few more tests."

I look over at Ander. His eyes are now blinking slowly, eyelids drooping. I watch him yawn and lean into Springer's side. "We'll bring him back in a few hours. He's tired."

Kane slowly turns toward us, a malicious look on her face. "I don't care if he's tired. I need to run more tests. You'll leave him here. Is that understood?"

Springer pulls me to his side, cutting off the ugly confrontation I was about to start. "We understand that you have more diagnostics to complete, but you can see that the kid is exhausted. So rather than creating a situation with a reluctant patient, let us take him for a few hours of rest."

Kane's eyes fall on Ander, and I see her lip curl in consternation before she relents. "I want him back in four hours."

Springer pipes in. "You'll get him in eight."

He pulls me out of the room and asks one of the guards standing by for directions to our new, larger quarters. We walk silently through the dimness. I want to unleash my frustration at this whole situation, but I bite my tongue, fuming inside, as we go through the twists and turns of the tunnels. Soon, Ander begins to lag and ends up needing to be carried the remainder of the way, his small head lolling against Springer's shoulder.

As we enter our quarters, I immediately notice a small cot has been placed between two others. It's not exactly a 'large' room as we had been led to believe, but it's big enough for all three of us to make do and be in some comfort. Our gear rests in the corner of the space. I'm happy to see that it appears no one has gone through any of it, not that I have much to speak of, but what I do have is mine. Springer squeezes through a gap between the mattresses and lays Ander down while I close the door behind us. It feels good to shut out the rest of the world. I sit on the edge of my bed and shrug out of my pack, letting it thump softy to the floor. Working the kinks out of my neck gives me time to reflect on this surreal situation before I open my mouth to unleash a torrent of complaints.

After Springer unloads his own gear, he stretches out on his bed, and I hear him let out a long sigh. "It's too late to change anything, Enora."

He always knows how to cut to the heart of the matter. "I know I can't change it." I snap at him and then feel badly immediately after. "I'm sorry, I don't mean to take it out on you. I don't like having this kid foisted off on us and not having any say about it. Plus, Dr. Kane really pissed me off. I don't like her. And I sure don't like the way she looks at Ander like he's a specimen she wants to dissect."

"I agree with you. The lady looks like she's been kept in that little room too long. But what do you want to do about it? It's not like we can go back."

I let out a frustrated breath. "I don't know what I want to do. I just know that I don't trust her. Honestly, I don't trust any of them."

"I don't either."

I'm surprised to hear this because lately, *I'm* the one who has trust issues, not him. It's unnerving to hear

Springer echo my suspicions and I wonder if there is any validity to our intuitions.

Springer slowly sits up and turns toward me. "The best we can do is watch and listen. If things get ugly, you and I will leave."

"Leave? Do you mean it?" I feel such hope at his statement. In that instant, a soft sigh comes from the little cot, and my gaze settles on the child. I have to force my mind to look beyond the mutation and truly see him. He's just a kid. It's not his fault he's here, stuck with us. It's ours. I watch his chest rise and fall in slumber. He looks so innocent. He *is* innocent. It's my anger that makes me resent him. No, it's not fair that he was cooked up in some lab and raised in the lap of luxury, but it's also not his fault. My shoulders slump.

"Springer, I can't leave him here." My voice sounds as defeated as I feel.

"What?"

I look up at Springer, forming the words I need to say. "Look, what do you think they would do to this kid if we left him here?" I watch as Springer's eyes fall on Ander's sleeping form. "Do you think they'd see him any differently than we do?"

"Enora..." He pauses, pinching his nose as he considers the situation. "You need to be reasonable. We couldn't take him with us. Do you have any idea how many people are already looking for this kid? If both sides were after him, we'd have no chance. None."

I know he's right, but I have to ignore that reality. "If we're forced to leave, he goes with us, or I don't go at all."

I hate giving an ultimatum but have no choice. It's like I'm grasping onto my last thread of humanity by pledging to protect this boy, this child that I stole and brought into a world that has its own agenda, one I do not fully understand yet. I look at Ander and suddenly see Safa's face, and then my parents. A wave of guilt washes over me. I left them behind. On a rational level, I know that I had no choice, but that is no comfort and doesn't ease the self-reproach that hammers my head. I left them to an awful fate. I'm not going to do that again.

Rather than continue to argue, I tell Springer, "Let's just wait and see. If all they want to do is show the world, then let them do it. We can look out for Ander and make sure they don't use him for anything else."

Springer gives me a hard look but capitulates in the end. I lie back onto my bed and let my mind go blank, listening to the soft breathing of a life that rests in my hands.

CHAPTER ELEVEN

Later that evening, we are at a table about to dig into our dinner rations. I've been eyeing my small portion with distaste since we sat down, ravenous but put off by the food itself. On my tray is a blob of cooked spinach and a cube of something that remotely resembles beef, though I know it's not. Only the privileged can eat real beef. There's no way I'd get any here. But this stuff doesn't look much like the processed substitute either. It's kind of grey and dry. I poke at it with my fork until Springer softly clears his throat. I look at him, and his eyes sweep the room.

I feel my face flame as I notice a small audience. Around us are inhabitants of this rebel faction, and many of them have taken note of my behavior. I wonder how many of these people stole the food I'm balking at in one of the near-constant raids that must occur to feed everyone stuck in this hole. As I look at some of the faces, I see a range of emotions from pity to resentment, more of them exhibiting the latter.

I cast my eyes at my plate and dig into the distasteful mess. At the very least, it'll assuage my constant hunger. I block out the hostility and choke down my food. I look longingly at my cup of water, wanting to chase down the gritty texture of the protein, but I need to savor it. That's the last ration I get until tomorrow.

Everyone's attention drifts from us when an announcement splashes across the live feed on the wall. It startles me to see my face, next to Springer's, with the words, *water traitors*, scrawling below our images. The captioning of the broadcast mentions nothing about Ander, and I wonder if that has been omitted because they don't know of our connection or if it's deliberate because they don't want the public asking questions about where he came from.

Ander's voice wrenches me out of my morbid fascination with the newscast when he says, "Enora, that's you!"

I'm so thankful that he doesn't try to read the scrolling list of our crimes. I swallow hard, feeling my spit get lodged in my throat, and end up coughing spastically. Ander pats my back until I regain control. My eyes are bleary from the episode, but I manage a smile and say, "Yep, that's me. I'm famous."

Ander beams, obviously pleased that he knows someone renowned, and digs into his bland dinner with single-mindedness. As he eats, my eyes wander over his tray. It seems like such a little thing, but I can't help noticing that the boy doesn't have any apparent interest in the small cup of water sitting untouched in the rounded corner of his platter. I look at it with some longing, always feeling a thirst that our rationing never quenches.

I turn my attention to Springer, whose eyes are still glued to the wall, reading the report displayed under our pictures. It's not a flattering account, and much of it contains blatant lies made to make the populace outraged and eager for our capture. Some of the claims are even punctuated with video of water tanks being destroyed, the contents gushing out and spilling onto the ground in an act of wastefulness that is sure to reach every heart who sees it. We have truly moved into the realm of outcast and rebel, an idea that I often talked of in the past but rarely thought I would partake in. For better or worse, I broke the shackles of complacency and am on my way to fulfilling my vow to Bram and my internal promise to Safa.

We eat our small meal quickly. I can avoid looking at the screen for the most part and focus on Ander's chatter. He talks too much for my taste. Or perhaps it's just that I'm not overly verbose and prefer the quiet. I wonder if all kids babble as much as he does or if this is just another quirk resulting from his genetic code. It's hard not to let it irritate me.

"You know what?" he says.

I really don't care, but humor him anyway. "What?"

"I know a secret." He drops his voice when he says this, and I immediately perk up, showing genuine interest.

"Oh?"

He nods and wriggles his hand at me to come closer. I lean in as he whispers, "I seen where the bad kids go. Miss Martha doesn't know, but I seen her take one of them. 'Cause you know how?"

I shake my head. "How?"

"I'm real good at sneaking, and I followed her and seen where they put him."

"Where was that?"

He cups his hand around his mouth, talking directly into my ear. "They took him to the bad place."

The bad place? I wonder what he means by that and can't help a small shudder as I recall the tomb of broken bones and tiny skulls. "Where is the bad place?"

"It's a big building, and it smells bad. We're not a'pposed to go there."

I'm having trouble piecing together what Ander is saying and don't want to just assume it's as awful as I'm imagining. "Miss Martha took your friend there? Did he come back?"

Ander gives me a look like I'm stupid. "Bad kids don't come back."

"Why not?"

"'Cause they're bad!"

"What makes them bad?" I push.

He cocks his head, thinking. "I don't know, lots of

things. Jago likes to hit and bite, so he got to go to the bad place, and he's not gonna come back. 'Cause they don't let you."

"Did he hit *you*?"

"No. I'm too fast, and he can't run so good. He hit Becca lots of times, though, and I saw him bite Miss Martha too. So, he's a bad kid."

I can see that he's getting weary of the conversation, so I back off, but questions are buzzing through my mind. Is this 'bad place' a type of behavior-programming center? Are there large percentages of kids who have violent traits? If so, is it a side effect of the mutation? Ander's attention has drifted back to his food, and Springer has completely ignored our exchange, having been glued to the screen. I want to get back to our quarters so I can fill him in and ask Ander more about this place he's talking about. Why is it that the kids don't come back? Inside, I feel like I know the answer to that question, and it's horrifying.

As we get up and leave the room, I feel the stares of a few eyes follow our progress and wonder at the emotions behind those gazes. I can't help feeling that the weight of some of those looks has an underlying malignant nature. Perhaps it is just my inherent skepticism, but I'm not convinced that everyone in this underground compound fully backs our actions or embraces us as equals. I grab onto Ander's hand, feeling an inexplicable need to show my proprietary feelings for him. It's hard to miss the faces that register my action. By showing such a public display, I feel that I've inadvertently thrown a gauntlet.

The three of us are making our way back to our quarters when Springer is stopped in the corridor and told to join Sergeant Quinn for a briefing. A pang of resentment flares as I acknowledge that I have intentionally been left out, but I force myself to let that anger go and take Ander back to our room. Once inside, I give him a few harmless gadgets to play with and impatiently wait for Springer to return.

Springer eventually opens the door to our room and indicates that I step outside. Keeping his voice low, he fills me in. "They are going to hack into the broadcasting system tomorrow morning during the daily newscast. The thinking is that the time frame will have the biggest audience."

This makes sense as I can recall the majority of broadcasts that I saw were in the morning or evening hours, and it is clearly too late for an evening bulletin now.

"Is Sergeant Quinn asking us to be a part of that broadcast?"

"No, she doesn't want us affiliated with it. She thinks that the recent news of our fugitive status would negatively influence anyone seeing the transmission."

"So, what does she want?"

"Ander."

I expected this, so it comes as no surprise. "Will she be

broadcasting the information I gathered along with stuff about Ander?"

"It's complicated. She knows that there will be a limited amount of time that they can successfully hack into the system before their transmission is shut down. So she plans to show pieces of what we found alongside Ander himself. Sergeant Quinn expects to have less than two minutes before the feed is disabled. Have you heard the stuff that Dr. Kane's tests revealed?"

"Yeah. It's pretty crazy." And it truly is something straight out of science fiction. Ander has such an advanced internal system that he can recycle his urine to diminish water loss. His body temperature fluctuates, reducing the amount of energy needed to maintain a constant 98.6 degrees like the rest of us. Plus, he doesn't seem to have tear ducts, and he produces less saliva than a regular human. And this is just has been found out up to now. I wonder what else could be lurking in his DNA.

I think over what the broadcast could actually tell people. A couple of minutes are not much time for people to make sense of what they are seeing. I assume that someone will also be narrating to ensure that anyone watching fully understands what he or she is looking at. The pessimist in me doesn't have much faith in the success of this endeavor, and I wager that we will need to do something more extreme to sway the public.

"What's the next step?"

"Sergeant Quinn has already reached out to other

factions, and they are collaborating to try to infiltrate facilities in their own areas in the hopes of corroborating what you found. If we can show people that this is not an isolated operation but a nationwide effort to create a new race and breed humans out, then she feels the resistance will have the power they need to build a rebellion and take down the DMC."

The plan is sound. Without a huge uprising, efforts will be wiped out in a blink. It is essential that people feel such anger that they are willing to revolt, no matter the cost. The price of the revolution is the hitch in this movement, though. The Company has control over every facet of daily life. They have the power to cut off all water and food to the general population. Naturally, this is a terrible threat and could lead to an immediate derailment of our efforts. Without gaining complete control of these resources, the Company could force entire communities to abandon any effort within days. Unlike these starving groups of rebels who have lived their entire lives with little to live on, civilians have been living lives of relative luxury, provided for at every turn, even though those provisions have been on the lighter side. Until joining this effort, I didn't truly understand what it meant to be hungry. Can the rest of the country go through that for a long time? Long enough to gain control?

I wonder how much thought these necessities have been given by the powers that be. "How is this a sustainable fight?"

"What do you mean?"

"Well, the Company has control over all resources. What's to stop them from cutting those resources off and letting people die of thirst?"

Springer nods. "I asked Sergeant Quinn the same question. In a staged effort, she's convinced that rebel divisions will gain control over water distribution and food production facilities. I'm not sure how that will work because there needs to be a presence to support the people in the towns and cities in addition to getting control over the compounds. Honestly, I don't think they have enough people to go around, and they certainly don't have the firepower and equipment to hold out for long in a full-blown attack."

I shake my head, frustrated by the apparent lack of forethought and the glaring possibility that this whole attempt is destined to fail with little to no impact on the DMC's operations and control. I begin to pace in small circles. Sergeant Quinn is a strong figure for her people but not overly impressive as a leader.

However, Commander Guire is a hulking beast of a man whose authority is stamped across his face and evident in every word or look he gives. He strikes me as a very competent strategist, and I can't imagine him not thinking through every minute detail of any effort.

But even with this, I feel like Springer has only been informed of part of the plan. I stop pacing. "There is something they're not telling you."

Springer looks at me. "What's that?"

"I'm not sure. But if what you say is true regarding the numbers, there has to be another operation going on at the same time that would somehow even the odds, or at least help the rebels, to take over the supplies."

"I don't think they're going to keep me appraised of that if there is another part of the plan that hasn't been shared."

"I don't either."

Eventually, we head back into the room, to Ander who is oblivious to our conversation and his part in this. I watch him playing quietly and wonder how important his role will be once it all begins in the morning. No matter how it plays out, this is just the beginning.

FOLLOWING AN EARLY MEAL OF A STALE PROTEIN BAR and a tiny cup of water, we make our way to the room that Sergeant Quinn has designated for the newscast. As we enter the cramped space, I see a camera set up opposite a wall that has been covered with a black cloth that acts as a background. It is an utterly undistinguishable room, in keeping with the anonymity of our location. Springer and I have told Ander that he will be on the morning announcement, just like he saw us the night before. Not understanding the significance of this, he's excited at the prospect.

The individuals who will be hacking into the system

to transmit our video feed are in another room. I'm shown where Ander needs to stand. Leaning down, I tell him he needs to be in front of the black cloth and that the camera will be on, recording him.

"Can I wave to Miss Martha?"

I look questioningly at the young woman behind the camera. She quickly steps out to pose the question to Sergeant Quinn and returns, shaking her head.

"You know what, Ander? Miss Martha isn't going to be watching this, so you need to just stand where I tell you and look at that camera."

He looks a bit crestfallen but quickly recovers, as the idea of being recorded is still exciting. "Okay. But I want to wave."

"I know you do, and maybe next time we can make sure that Miss Martha is watching, and you can wave then, okay?"

He gives me a grin and nods.

A few minutes later, we are given the signal to begin recording. Ander stands still, looking directly at the camera.

Dr. Kane narrates the video displayed on a small screen next to me, and I'm surprised with how powerful her message is.

"This is Ander. He may look like a normal child, but he was born in a lab, a genetic mutation created by the DMC to replace your children. He is an example of what the DMC calls: the Aurora Strain. This child has been specially designed to flourish in our world. His yellow eyes are the most noticeable feature. They are strange and frightening. If you look closer, you will see his peculiar skin is covered by a waxy secretion that helps his body trap the water." As she says this, an image of a close-up of Ander's skin is displayed next to his form. "But it is inside his body that we see the biggest differences between this aberration and humans. Mutations, like this child, have been specially designed for this world. These beings are the future in the eyes of the DMC." A brief list of information pops up next to Ander. In it, I can see the list of internal mutations that all result in his remarkable ability to use less water.

I'm impressed that Ander's able to stand relatively still throughout the recording, fidgeting only slightly as the seconds tick by. Almost a minute in, I see his hand begin to rise as though about to wave. He looks at me, and I shake my head, mouthing a silent no. His nose scrunches, but he puts his hand down.

"Don't let the DMC continue to lie to you," Dr. Kane's voice continues. "They are planning to replace your children with ones like this boy. The Aurora Strain will be all that is left, and we will be extinct in the future. You cannot let this happen! Join the resistance! Rise up and fight the power trying to systematically wipe us out! The DMC is not your friend. They have been lying to you. Join us!"

The recording ends, and after a quick perusal, it's given the proverbial thumbs up. Behind the scenes, the tech specialists, run by a man named Dade, finalize the video and upload it into the DMC's morning broadcast. As a result, it's looped twice before being cut off.

The Company has probably latched onto that signal and is attempting to trace it to the location of origin. There must be a handful of people from the inside working to block that effort. It's frightening to imagine the outcome if the resistance is not successful in keeping this place secret. Already, drones and DMC scouting parties have made numerous sweeps across the state trying to locate rebel factions. I know from whispered conversations that these patrols have had a huge impact in various divisions conducting necessary food and water raids. Up to now, we've been lucky, but I know that transmitting the video will increase DMC's presence. While I don't enjoy the food, it's sure nice to have some.

I am hopeful the short video provided enough information to make people aware and willing to take action. It's strange to think that this small block of time could result in a wave of resistance. Perhaps, the tide is turning.

CHAPTER TWELVE

Twenty men and women, many of them too young, are chosen to go to the nearby town of Springfield, the location of most of the food raids. The goal is to assist with the small uprising that took place shortly after the video transmission in the hope of gaining control of the town. The mood is jubilant as the team of rebels gear up to leave, though Springer is irritated at having been told to stay behind. I feel somewhat ambivalent about it. Part of me wants to go, but the loudest part wants to use the success of this effort to get permission to find the lake Bram told us about. I long to see a body of water like that, to realize part of a dream and share it with the world.

The skirmish in Springfield makes it possible to leave the rebel compound and go above ground as DMC forces are focused on squashing the rebellion. Springer and I head to the surface with the bulk of the community. It feels good to stand in the sun. I don't even mind the dry heat. My body absorbs the warmth, and I look down at my arm, imagining I'll be able to see vitamin D soaking into my skin. What I see instead makes me cringe. Dirt and grime, barely visible in the dim lights underground, are glaringly evident under the harsh light of day. I'm not a neat freak or anything, but it's tough to realize how grungy I am. Showers, or quick sponge baths like I used to do in Prineville, are not possible anymore. This is another stark reminder of how life outside DMC control is so different.

My attention is drawn to a flurry of activity when five beat-up jeeps drive by carrying the rebel forces. Through the open windows, I see faces wreathed in smiles and arms extended, pumping rifles into the air. The air of excitement is contagious.

I look over at Springer, who is standing silently next to me. My grin falters when I take in his expression. "What's wrong?"

He shakes his head. "I should be with them. Sergeant Quinn put Reid in charge, and he's too cocky, always trying to prove himself when I train with him."

I search my memories for Reid but come up blank. "Have I met him?"

"Nope. He avoids the dining hall, preferring to eat with a handful of his followers who seem to think he's hot shit."

"Oh." I'm not sure what else to say. I've been so

distracted with Ander and everything that we've been preparing for that I hadn't thought to ask how the few training sessions he's been running have gone.

"It'll probably be fine. I just know I could do a better job of keeping those kids safe."

"I'm sorry you can't be with them, Springer."

"Thanks."

I watch as he wanders off a ways to speak with Sergeant Quinn. Scanning the area, I see that Ander has found Hal, and the two of them are busy digging in the dirt. It's easy to see that Hal used to be a father. He's got 'Dad' written all over him, and he's clearly enamored with Ander. As I watch the two of them together, I take a good look at the boy. In the sunlight, his skin looks luminescent, as though whatever his skin secretes reflects some of the light. It's not terribly noticeable, but knowing how different he is, I see it.

Most of us stay outside for a couple of hours, but the heat eventually drives us underground. Not having large water rations really takes a toll. I don't remember getting so faint in the past, and I think it must be because of the severe rationing. I pin so much hope on the success of this revolt. There will be so much to go around if we get control of Springfield. I can't help the visions of food as they tumble through my mind. Part of me misses my old role.

. . .

ONLY TWO JEEPS AND SEVEN PEOPLE RETURN THAT evening. One young soldier, maybe 15, is carried out of the back of a vehicle, bloodied arms hanging limply. His mouth is slack, and his breathing is shallow as he's brought to Dr. Kane. In my heart, I know he won't make it. The faces of the others are haunted, and the once jubilant mood of the community is gone, swallowed by despair.

"What happened?" I ask Springer after he returns from a debriefing with Sergeant Quinn.

Springer looks around our room. "Where's Ander?"

"He's with Hal. I thought it would be better if he wasn't around to overhear anything."

"Good."

I wait as he settles onto his cot, wiping his hands across his face in a way I've seen too many times before. "Did the boy die too?"

"Yeah. They lost fourteen people today. Ten of them shouldn't have even been there. They were kids who were really trained to get in and out of places during raids. They weren't prepared for a fight."

I can see the anger and frustration radiating from him. "What about Reid?"

"Dead, though I can't say I'm too sorry about that. It's his fault so many never made it back."

"How so?"

"Springfield is one of their primary locations for food raids, so they're pretty familiar with the layout of the town. They've got some secret way in and out, and Reid decided they use it to break into the town. It would've worked too if he hadn't been so overconfident." He shakes his head in frustration.

"Did the Company know they were coming?"

"No. But there should've been a distractor of some kind so that the rebels could use their access point relatively undiscovered. But Reid decided to go in guns blazing. One jeep didn't even make it past the perimeter, but the other three got into the town and somehow managed to avoid getting blown to hell. They were able to take cover and met up with a small group of the townspeople who had started the whole uprising. But Reid, being the smug asshole that he was, took command of everything, and that's when it all went to hell."

The picture Springer paints is not a pretty one, the losses on all sides being an ugly part of this war. I listen as he describes how the battle escalated and finally turned in the DMC's favor when a large group of men and women leading the rebellion were killed in an aerial bombing of the building they had been using as their base. Reid was among them. After that, the remaining soldiers from our division retreated, somehow making it out in the haze of smoke that covered their departure. I think the loss of so many is catastrophic to this place as I listen to Springer wrap up the details.

"If Sergeant Quinn had just let me go, I could've organized our troops, and we would have control of the town."

"You can't know that for sure, Springer. The resistance

is made up of people who lack training, supplies, and equipment. We're trying to fight a power that has every resource at its fingertips. I doubt the outcome would've been as clear-cut as you're imaging if you had been allowed to lead them."

"I know, but if our efforts weren't being led by someone with more courage than sense..." He doesn't finish his thought.

"I'm sorry you weren't there. Or at least part of me is. The other part is relieved that you were nowhere near the fighting."

Springer gives me a tight smile. "Yeah."

Food rations are tightened immediately. Breakfast the next morning consists of half the food that we normally receive. Water rations show no change, but these were already extreme, and without enough water, we'd all be useless anyway. I feel the glares as the three of us sit down to eat. We are taking food from the mouths of the people who've lived here their whole lives. I feel self-conscious with each bite and chew the bland reconstituted eggs and hard cracker as quickly as possible.

"I'm still hungry," Ander pipes up. I look at him and watch as he pops every crumb he can find into his mouth.

I give him the last half of my cracker, trying not to feel resentful as my stomach snarls in dissatisfaction.

The transmission and the rebels' efforts in this division

have not had the desired effect. While small pockets of dissent arose in other areas, the backlash is swift and severe. We learn that numerous executions occur in public squares, an inevitable result, though nonetheless sickening. These spectacles have their desired effect, and resistance fades quickly before even taking a full breath. As we leave the dining hall, I feel the tension and sense misplaced blame as people look at Ander with accusation. I am careful not to show any reaction to their condemnation, but I take careful note of where it comes from.

By that afternoon, the DMC launches a counterattack across the airwaves. Springer and I are meeting with Sergeant Quinn to discuss another, more powerful broadcast of Ander when the DMC's message lights up the regular programming that has been playing quietly on a large screen in the background. Sergeant Quinn turns up the volume, and we move toward the screen, watching the grainy image of General Malvolia.

"Dear citizens. As you know, traitors have launched attacks on our democracy. Through illegal transmissions, they have spread lies and sowed fear. I am here to tell you that these radical groups have one goal: war on our country and our way of life. The insurgents leading this group of extremists are attempting to convince you that the DMC is covering up a plan to create a new race of people. This is science fiction. These are lies.

The DMC was created to preserve human life, not replace or destroy it. For the last one hundred years, our organization has saved millions and worked hard to protect resources for future generations. We, at the DMC, live among you. We are part of your towns and cities. We are here to protect you from these vicious attacks. Do not be fooled by the propaganda of these fanatics. They are not trying to free you from imagined oppression. They are trying to enslave you, and your children, by destroying our democracy.

It is time for us to do our part to protect our communities. If you see a traitor, you must report him. If you hear traitorous speech, you must report it. Together we can keep our families and our way of life safe from these terrorists."

The broadcast ends with a large image of the DMC symbol overlaid by a message I have heard many times.

The room is silent as the image and message bleed out of the screen, and regular programming resumes.

Sergeant Quinn breaks the silence. "We will need to

respond quickly and with a powerful message. Enora, please get Ander and take him to Dr. Kane. I want to know if there is any other data she needs that would be useful as we move forward."

"Yes, ma'am."

Her dismissal puts me off. Clearly, Springer is allowed to stay and be part of whatever plans are discussed. It's irritating that I'm given the role of babysitter. I stomp through the passages, muttering to myself and wishing that I were anywhere but here in this grungy, smelly hole with nothing to eat. By the time I reach my room, where Hal has been taking care of Ander, the heat of my anger has dimmed.

Dr. Kane is in deep conversation with a man I have met only briefly when Ander and I arrive. His name escapes me, but I recognize his stringy hair and pocked face. As I stand in the doorway with Ander, they glance at us in annoyance. Leaning into Kane, the man whispers something, making her laugh and shake her head. I settle for giving them both a cold stare while I bite back the words that are itching to come out. I don't want to make enemies, but it's getting hard to reign in my anger, and I worry that soon I won't care if I let something fly. For now, I listen to my inner reasoning.

Finally, they wrap up their little dialogue, and the man strolls toward the door, an ugly sneer on his face. "Excuse me, can you move aside? I don't want to brush up against *that*."

I arch an eyebrow at him and don't move an inch. My grip tightens on Ander, keeping him in place. It's just like high school again, except Ander's the 'pleb' and this guy's the drone, only he's just as ugly on the inside as he is on the outside. When the man sees I'm not moving, he roughly pushes me aside and huffs through the doorway. I can't help shoving back and grin in sick pleasure when his thin shoulder jams into the doorframe, causing him to yelp. He mutters something under his breath and stalks down the passageway.

I hear Kane chuckling. "You know, you really don't want to get on Zeke's bad side."

"I don't care to be on his good side either." I snap at her.

That stops her laughter. "That's your prerogative, but you're making a mistake."

I shrug. "Sergeant Quinn asked us to come by to see if you needed any additional data."

"Put it on the cot. I'd like to get more measurements."

I don't miss the reference. So, Kane and Zeke, and others of their ilk, think of Ander as a thing. 'It' she said, and I can only assume that label was an intentional warning. She doesn't see Ander as a living, feeling child. I will need to be more watchful of what goes on with the boy. If Kane's opinion is shared by many people here, then Ander will be an easy target.

I walk over and hoist the boy up, setting him down a bit too roughly, my annoyance still coursing through my veins. I pause, hands still on his waist, while I collect myself. When I'm under control again, I pat him gently, trying to reassure him that I'm not mad. He's been uncharacteristically quiet this entire time and looks up at me with a hint of fear on his face. His look acts as a slap, making me instantly remorseful.

I force a smile and say softly, "Dr. Kane just wants to do a few more things, okay?"

He only nods and glances at Kane, who comes over with a device I've never seen before in her hand. "Hold out your arm."

The boy obeys, and I watch as the device clamps down, biting into his tender skin. Ander yelps and tries to pull his arm away.

"Hold still!" Kane barks and then repositions the equipment.

I reach behind Ander and take hold of his arm, trying to keep him in place so that we can get this over with.

"It'll be over soon," I promise.

Kane takes readings of Ander's arms and legs, jotting down notes with numbers that have no meaning as I look at them. Finally, she puts the device down, and I reach over to pick Ander up and leave.

"I'm not finished yet."

I look at Kane in confusion. "How much more do you need to do?" I can see the child is getting anxious, and I'm afraid the strange, tearless crying is going to start, and I have no idea how to deal with that.

Kane huffs in annoyance. "That was for his extremities. I need data on his torso as well. Lay him down."

I pause, oddly reluctant to do as she asks. Why am I feeling so protective? It doesn't make sense. Ander is a tool, not even a real child. Yet I can't help the unfamiliar feelings that leap to the surface when I sense that Kane's test may cause more discomfort. Hearing the boy in pain does something to me, and I don't like it. I fight an inner battle with my conscience but eventually rein these feelings in and gently push Ander down so that he is flat on the cot.

I end up having to hold him down. It doesn't take long for him to start squealing as Kane pinches and prods, pulls, and bends. I watch Ander struggle and whimper under Kane's dispassionate glare, and that unwelcome feeling grows, fed by the cries that pull at a part of me I am struggling to smother.

When Kane draws blood after Ander wiggles, I lose it. "Okay, stop. We're done." I roughly pull Ander off the cot and swing his little body behind me, grabbing his shirt and stuffing it in my pocket.

Kane tries to snatch the boy by snaking her arm around my side. I shove her backward, and she catches herself on the edge of the cot. "Sergeant Quinn will hear about this."

"Good."

I drag Ander out of the room, so mad that I can't even

talk. He's silent at my side, little legs struggling to keep up as we eat up the distance to our room.

When we get there, I jerk the door open and slam it once we're inside. Ander is shaking. I can feel him trembling as I motion for him to sit on his bed. I take a minute to breathe deeply, working to calm myself down. When I finally feel the adrenaline leave my limbs, and my heart slow to a normal rhythm, I let out a slow gush of air.

I sit down next to Ander, who shies away from me. It hurts a little to see him do this. "I'm not mad at you, Ander," I sigh in frustration.

He slowly moves toward me, and I reach out, feeling unsure what to do. I pat his head and then want to roll my eyes because he's not a dog or something. I settle for resting my arm around his shoulders and am relieved when he scoots closer, snuggling up against my side.

Ander's eyes look hurt, and he is hiccuping softly, hand reaching toward mine like a lifeline as he rests against my side. I feel guilt settle in my gut as I look down at him. I know I should pay more attention to him. It's not his fault that he's here and that he's stuck with me. I feel his weight sink into my side, and a part of me wants to pull away. But there's another side of myself, one I've kept buried under layers of self-preservation, which feels the urge to pull him closer. As I battle these two sides of myself, questions spin through my mind. How many other children will be stolen because of our actions? Aberrations or not, they are innocent of any wrongdoing and have become expendable pawns in this burgeoning war.

Did we do the right thing?

I want to talk to Springer about it, but I've been strangely reluctant to broach the subject. Honestly, I'm a little embarrassed that I have any true feelings for Ander. I know I need to keep my objectivity. He's a tool to bring the DMC down and expose them for what they are. But, if I give in to any misguided maternal feelings, then I'm putting everything at risk. So, I must face the cold reality that I need to put my energy into building a wall around my heart, one that a few whimpers won't be able to break down next time.

CHAPTER THIRTEEN

Springer and I are in the briefing room with Sergeant Quinn and the new leader of her troops, a man named Donovan, when the next transmission is sent. Nasty thoughts pop into my head of the painful measurements that Dr. Kane said she needed as I realize Ander wasn't part of this video. Now it seems that the whole episode was just a means to hurt the boy. It fills me with disgust to think that's all she wanted to do. Even a mutation feels pain. And he's still human, part of him at least.

Instead of Ander's presence, images of the women, those inhuman vessels that birth his kind, fill the screen. It is horrifying all over again, seeing their bloated bodies and slack mouths. Next come pictures of dead infants, poor deformed beings who lived to take a breath before being destroyed. Overlaid in the unsettling communication is a narrative warning civilians of the DMC's goal of replacing their children with monstrosities. The transmission manages to be run only once before the feed is cut.

Sergeant Quinn looks smug at the success of the broadcast. "I need everyone to prepare for a new wave of resistance. Springer, you will assist Donovan in the training of our newest soldiers."

"I can get started immediately."

"Good. Why don't you and Donovan gather them up and begin? We may need everyone ready by tomorrow."

The two men leave, and I am left standing there, unsure where to go or what to do. "Enora, I'd like you to work with a small team of two and train them in the use of the mapping and surveillance equipment. Specifically, I need you to sufficiently train at least one individual who can assist you in securing and monitoring a location in any upcoming operations."

"Yes, ma'am. I will do what I can, though you know that the equipment here is limited. And I can't teach specifics about the DMC security systems without being able to access them."

"I understand. My main goal is for you to have support during any future raids or attacks. I want one of my people to be able to monitor a location while you are working within the DMC system. Do you think that's feasible?"

"Absolutely," I assure her. "Did you have specific individuals in mind?"

"I think you will find Farrel and Corin to be apt candidates."

"Thank you. I'll get started." I leave the room and head to a storage area where I have spent some time cataloging equipment. It's a pretty sad collection, truth be told. But considering where I am, it's not surprising that many of the devices are beyond repair. A few work relatively well, and I grab these and head to the common area where most of the community can be found when not working. I expect Farrel and Corin to be there and will probably be painfully young to do anything like what I'll be training them for.

The decrepit area everyone in this place uses as a social hub has only a handful of people in it when I come out of an offshoot leading to the room. It's a rounded area, more of an intersection of sorts, with benches made from scraps lining the cement floor in a sad imitation of a public square. The only positive thing I note is that the smell is less oppressive here. Maybe it has something to do with the airflow from multiple tunnels leading into and out of the space. Like everywhere else, it's dim, the yellow lighting casting a glow in pockets but never really illuminating all of it. It's probably better that there isn't much light here or anywhere in this place because I shudder to think of the muck I might see.

As I scan the room, I can see a couple of small clusters of young people and assume the two I am looking for are among them. I'm walking toward the closest group when it occurs to me that I don't see the handful of elderly who usually spend their time here. I pause and scan the room again, thinking I may have missed them, but they are nowhere. It's strange and makes me feel uneasy for reasons I can't explain.

Continuing, I step up to a group of four kids. That's what they are. Children. My heart sinks as I glance at the other group and see that the ages are about the same. I want to turn around and leave, but Sergeant Quinn has given me her orders.

I clear my throat. "Hey." All eyes, from both groups, swivel to me. "I'm Enora. I've seen most of you around but haven't had a chance to meet you face to face."

One young man, maybe sixteen and the eldest of all of them, steps forward with his hand out. "Enora, I'm Farrel. You're a Pathfinder, right?"

I want to cringe when he says this with such enthusiasm and awe. "Yeah. I mean, I was before I joined the resistance."

Farrel smiles and turns his grin on his friends, clearly impressed. Like so many people down here, Farrel is skinny, with gangly limbs covered in a layer of grime. His height gives him an appearance of awkward youthfulness, and I hope he's not the clumsy type. He's got a handsome face, despite his pale thinness.

He looks down at me with admiration stamped across his features. "That's really cool. I'd love to be able to do something like that someday. You know, to help my community."

"It's funny you should say that, Farrel because I came here looking for you. Sergeant Quinn would like me to train you and Corin."

He hops up in excitement and whoops. "Hey, Corin," He hollers as he looks behind me at the other group of kids who made their way over as I began talking. "Did you hear what she said?"

A girl, even younger than Farrel, steps toward us shyly, looking at me. Her hair is lank and dirty, plaited into two braids on either side of her head. She's about my height, though lack of good food and sunlight makes her look unhealthy and very young.

"Did you say you're going to train Farrel and me?" Her quiet voice asks.

I want to tell them I've changed my mind, but that choice isn't mine to make like so many things in my life. "Yep. I'd like to get started right away. Sergeant Quinn needs at least one of you to be ready as soon as possible."

"I'm ready to go," Farrel pipes up, his excitement clear.

Corin's response is more reserved. "Okay. I'm ready too."

They say a quick goodbye to their friends, and I lead them up to the surface where we can get a good look at the equipment and begin to use it.

As we walk, I ask the question that has been niggling

in the back of my mind since I found these two. "Where are those older people I always see in the commons?"

Corin turns away, her lips smashing into a hard line. I look at Farrel and see a shadow pass over his face before he answers softly. "They were taken away after we lost so many in the uprising."

"Taken where?"

He shrugs. "I don't know, just away. They won't be coming back."

I can feel how uncomfortable they are, so I don't press for more information. I don't need to anyway. With the loss of the bulk of the men and women who did much of the raiding, food is even scarcer. In a place like this, hard choices are the only ones to make.

"I'm sorry." There's nothing more I can say.

I don't ask any more questions, and we soon find ourselves at a juncture that leads above ground. I go up the ladder first, pulling on a lever to open the panels above. There is a low grinding sound as they pull away, revealing a rectangular portal to the surface. Motioning for Farrel and Corin to stay behind, I climb out. The glare of the sun is blinding, but it feels so good. When my eyes adjust, I scan the sky for drones and then walk out and look in all directions for any sign of DMC vehicles. There's nothing out here today. I lean back into the hole and shout for my new trainees to head on up.

I spend the next few hours going over the basics. The two of them are eager students, but it's clear that Corin has my instincts from the start. She latches onto the mapping system as though born for this analytical work. Farrel shows more aptitude with a surveillance-type role, and I decide that I will tell Sergeant Quinn that I need them both. At least that way, they can keep an eye out for each other if I have to take them with me in a future operation.

Halfway through the day, we stop and go to the dining hall. While my stomach is aching in an empty, nauseating way, I am reluctant to go below ground, into the darkness and the stink. But I don't want to seem ungrateful for the little I'm being given, so I follow Corin and Farrel, listening to their excited chatter as we join the others.

Springer is already there, with Ander and Hal, when I walk into the room. As I grab my ration and head to the table, I hear whispered conversation and see covert glances shooting in my direction. I want to roll my eyes, but I practice restraint and keep a straight face.

I sit next to Springer and lean forward to see Ander on his other side. "Hey, guys."

Ander, who had been playing a clapping game with Hal, looks over at me. "Hi, Enora. Hal's been teaching me games. Wanna see?"

"Sure do."

He engages in a series of complicated claps against Hal's hands that form a rhythm. After one round, they speed up and continue to do so until Ander falters and ends up in a fit of giggles. Seeing him laugh lightens my mood.

I look at Springer, who's been watching along with me. "How's it going with your group?"

He gives a half-hearted laugh. "Let's just say, I've got my work cut out for me. If any of them are over twenty, I'd be shocked. They're just a bunch of kids. They can load a gun, and their aim is pretty good, but they don't have the stomach for what they've been trained to do."

"Yeah."

Springer looks at me. "I don't know how we can get them ready in time. If Sergeant Quinn is right, and uprisings begin again, these kids won't be much help."

"I know. I'm working with two myself, a fourteen and fifteen-year-old. They're too young to be doing this, but there's no one else."

That's the biggest problem. Since we lost so many in Springfield, the remaining adults have been reassigned to be part of raiding parties. But, they haven't seen much success. The DMC has increased patrols and security, which has made the last two raids unsuccessful. If they can't get supplies, I don't know how long everyone can survive down here.

As always, the wall screen is running DMC programming in the background as we wrap up our meager meal. So I'm not surprised when I see a message pop up. It's General Malvolia again, but there is raw footage of different towns and cities this time.

"Dear Citizens," Her strong voice begins. The room goes quiet, and someone turns up the volume so we can all hear. "Terrorists are targeting our homes and families. These traitors are spreading lies with doctored photos and fabricated stories of experimentation. While these disturbing lies have distracted many of us, extremists have taken advantage, systematically attacking our supply lines and production facilities. The result of these attacks is felt across the state." The general's image shifts to the corner, and footage of citizens fill the screen. They look lost and hungry.

"These are the faces of the people who are being hurt by the radicals who are attacking our freedom. Men, women, and children are going hungry while traitors steal and destroy." Every statement is corroborated with footage of attacks on everything from supply trucks to water depots. "Do not be fooled by their lies. The rebels are not here to help you. They do not care about your families. These people want to destroy your way of life. They are envious of all you have and will not be satisfied until you and your children are left starving.

Remember, citizens, if you see a traitor, you must report him. If you hear traitorous speech, you must report it. Together we can keep our families and our way of life safe from these terrorists."

As before, the transmission ends with the DMC symbol and message. However, the quiet doesn't last long. Soon people around us stand up and begin yelling. There is a contagious energy in the room, and I find myself joining them, smiling at Ander and Springer as they, too, shout for revolution.

IN PREPARATION FOR THE WAVE OF RESISTANCE Sergeant Quinn anticipates, Springer asks to join our troops. But Springer's request is denied. Not being allowed to join in a fight rubs him the wrong way, and I can see him chafe at the refusal.

"This is crap," he mutters as he enters our room, throwing his gear on his bed that evening.

"What's their excuse?"

"Apparently, I'm too valuable to their agenda to be allowed to fight." His tone is laced with condescension. "Quinn says if either of us is captured or killed, the other factions could pull back their efforts. She's not willing to risk it."

"I don't see how we could be that important."

He cracks his neck, lets out an irritated sigh, and plops onto his bed. "I don't either. It's just an excuse."

"Maybe we know too much, Springer."

"Yeah, maybe we do."

I don't know how to feel about all of this. On the one hand, I'm relieved that Springer isn't out there risking his life when I won't be there to watch his back. But I also recognize that we can't just stay here in the shadows, part of this but not part of it. Even here, among people fighting for what we believe, we are outsiders. I look over at Ander, who is curled on his side under a worn blanket. He doesn't belong here either. I wonder what this could mean, if it means anything.

Springer's mood is palpable. I look at him and see the tension and the anger. "Do you think they'll let us out of here soon? On another assignment or anything?"

"I doubt it, Enora."

I grimace, imagining spending the rest of my life down here. It's easy to picture myself succumbing to persistent control and losing who I am. As I focus on these morbid thoughts, it occurs to me that I have no more freedom here than I did aboveground. In fact, I would have to say that I have less, especially since we kidnapped Ander. His presence is like an anchor, tying us to a life no better than where we came from. Knowing how these thoughts will spiral into nastiness, I mentally shake myself and stand up.

I begin to pace, thinking of what Springer said. "If we are part of whatever plans they are making, what do you think our role will be? It can't just be to hole up down here doing nothing but training the next crop of freedom fighters."

"No, I don't think that's their plan. Don't get me wrong. They need all the help they can get with this group of kids they are trying to mold into an army. But I get the feeling that whatever they are thinking to do with us long term is connected to Ander. Why else would he be solely our responsibility?"

He feels just as trapped as I am. "You're probably right.

I'm just not sure what they want us to do with him. Maybe take him to different outposts and drum up support?" The moment I suggest the idea, it sounds incredibly appealing. We could get out of this underground prison if that were the plan.

Springer shrugs. "I don't know, maybe."

Eventually, he rolls over, and I tire of pacing. At least sleep will help while away the hours.

As it turns out, there is no uprising, people having already been traumatized by the brutal reaction of the Company after the last one. I wonder what this will mean for us.

The days crawl by, frustratingly slow and monotonous. I spend my time training Corin and Farrel, Ander either joining me or off with Springer or Hal. Sergeant Quinn provides vague briefings during, letting us know of successful raids and secret meetings with factions of resistance within towns, but never giving us too many specifics. The communications delivered to the masses have sent small shockwaves through communities, but people are wary of revolting against such a powerful force. It's obvious that our images and data are not the catalysts the resistance thought they would be. People are too scared, too dependent on an entity that has made it impossible to be anything but entirely reliant on them. I wonder if that apathy would change if they knew the DMC hid a lake that could easily sustain tens of thousands.

Throughout all of this, multiple pockets of resistance

have attempted to breach various cities, to look for subdivisions like Renascence, and none have been successful. Our breach was an unprecedented infiltration that likely put any other facility on full alert. In all honesty, I am not sure how many more places like Renascence there are. I only presume there must be more. Without additional examples of the work going on behind the DMC, gathering a true force to fight their power is a daunting task.

It seems that we need something more shocking to get people motivated to fight.

Ghosts
both new and old,
Reach their wraith-like hands
Into the heart
Wrenching us
From what we are
And what we know
The dead speak
With the desperation
Of the living

CHAPTER FOURTEEN

It is footage that I had not been aware they had, having been kept ignorant of any part of it. The broadcast airs during an evening series of announcements. I sit with Ander and Springer in the dining hall, watching the typical Company programming when it interrupts the newscast.

There's an aerial view of a town, much like Prineville. I can see the usual buildings and housing units scattered throughout and can even make out people moving about the town. The narration begins by describing the community of Bristol with its population of about three thousand. There seems to be a gathering in the central part of the town as there are numerous people clustered outside what I assume is the municipal center. It looks like a benign assembling, as I can't make out any skirmishes and anything that could be construed as confrontational. The camera pans away from the crowd and drifts to what looks like a playground, perhaps outside of a school, as there is a large building adjacent to it. I can make out blurry images climbing on the equipment and running around.

As I watch the scene, the image suddenly blooms into a ball of white fire. It is blindingly bright, and I avert my gaze to escape the flood of brilliance. When the glare recedes seconds later, the playground is nothing but blobs of fire and twisted metal. The camera turns slowly, showing flattened buildings and unidentifiable charred remains of things my mind shies away from.

As I watch, in horror, the aftermath continues to unfold while the narrator goes on. The audience is told the recent footage was stolen in an effort to tell the world the truth of how the DMC deals with those who resist. According to the narrator, the groups of people gathered in the video were in their second day of peaceful protest after watching the information recently broadcast by the resistance. The voice goes on to state that no participants were armed or aggressive. Rather than giving voice to potential pockets of dissent, the DMC has eliminated it entirely. It is a warning from this powerful entity. It is a call to arms.

My mouth hangs open in shock after the communication is cut off and the regular programming resumes, followed by someone at another table turning it off completely. I note the multitude of gasps around me rolling through the room. That could have been my town. Those could have been my parents trying to calmly fight for their freedom from a power that has always kept them under rigid control. I turn to Springer and see my disbelief mirrored in his face. Realistically, since we made our discovery in Renascence, I've known that the DMC views the bulk of the population as a lesser investment than those like Ander. But it is a hard pill to swallow when you see such callous disregard for our lives on a large scale.

I can only hope that such a vile display of retribution will be the impetus people need to rip the blinders off and see the Company for what it really is. Springer and I need to prepare. This is our fight. No matter how Sergeant Quinn wants to utilize our standing within the resistance movement, I will not stand idly by while others mobilize and confront the enemy.

My feelings are echoed throughout the room as others stand and begin to shout, "Revolution!"

I feel a surge of power radiating throughout my body as I listen to the chant grow in volume and feeling. Springer and I stand and join the chorus, pumping our fists in the air. The energy in the room is contagious, and while I'm sucked into the fury, I become oblivious to the small form cowering in the chair next to me. I have utterly forgotten about Ander as I lend my voice to the hum of rebellion. But others have not forgotten him or what he represents.

A woman with a sneer plastered across her face charges over and roughly grabs Ander out of his chair, swinging him into the air and shaking him roughly. He cries out in fear. All the while, she is screaming for revolution. Seeing this, I experience a flood of rage like nothing I have felt before. I stalk over, cock my fist and slam it into her face with such force that her body is propelled backward, crashing into the table behind her. As she falls, I snatch Ander from her suddenly slack arms and swing him onto my back.

My voice comes out as a nasty snarl as I step toward the flailing woman and spit out, "You ever touch him again, and I'll kill you."

I let my eyes sweep a room that is suddenly swamped in stunned silence, giving everyone within my gaze the same warning. Then, I charge from the room and head to our quarters. I give no thought to Springer as I make my way through the tunnels, knowing he will try to diffuse the situation if he can and then join me.

The ferocity that made my heart race is now leaving my body, and I feel the receding adrenaline in tremors throughout my limbs. The subtle shaking mirrors Ander's small trembles as he tightens his grip around my neck to balance himself as we walk. I pat his hands, not trusting my voice until I calm down. As soon as we make it to our room, I shut the door and drop him gently onto his cot, scooting his legs over so I can join him. Now that we are away from all of the drama, I feel a sense of calm wash over me and find my voice.

"I'm sorry that lady grabbed you like that."

"She was scary." His voice is so small as he whispers this.

"I know. I'm sorry I didn't stop her in time."

"Why was everybody yelling? Were they mad?"

"Yes, but not at you."

Ander crawls onto my lap, fitting his arms around my waist, and I know I am forgiven. I pat his back, unsure how I should comfort him and calm his fears after such a traumatic event. I'm not even sure why I want to or where these feelings are coming from.

It's such a foreign emotion to want to care for someone else, to be responsible for their well-being. For this emotion to surface with *this child* is even more disconcerting. Ander isn't even human, not in the sense that I am. It feels like I'm betraying my race to feel compassion and righteous anger on his behalf. But I can't help it. Ander has wheedled his way past my defenses, and it's time that I stop lying to myself and pretend otherwise.

So stop trying to fight it. I care about him. It's as simple as that. It's a strange sensation when I do this, almost like I can feel the wall I've built, to insulate myself, come crumbling down. There's a brief flare of warning, my subconscious mind trying to put up one last defense to protect me, and then it's gone. I am laid bare with this new reality.

Ander's body relaxes after a few minutes, and his arms loosen. Then, he pulls away to look at my face.

"How come that lady wanted to hurt me? I didn't do nothing to her."

I sigh, struggling to find the right words to explain that she didn't want to hurt him, even though it sure seemed that way. "She wasn't trying to hurt you. I know she was too rough, but she was just excited. Sometimes people get carried away and don't realize what they're doing."

Ander nods at this, clearly making some connection. "Fiona hurt me sometimes, but I know she didn't mean to."

"Who's Fiona?"

"She's my friend. Sometimes she gets mad and hits me, but I know she doesn't mean it."

"We all do things we don't mean. I'm sure she felt bad, though." His statement reminds me of the 'bad kids' like Jago that he told me he went to the bad place and never returned. I'm tempted to ask if the same thing happened to Fiona but decide to drop it.

"Yeah." Ander wipes his nose on the back of his hand, and I'm glad to see that he is getting over the whole episode. "Can I play with the toy you gave me?"

"Sure."

I lean over and grab it for him, then get up and open the door, peeking into the hall, hoping to see Springer. I stand there for a few minutes and am finally rewarded by his slow gait coming toward me. I look back at Ander to make sure he's occupied and then shut the door behind me so that Springer and I can talk privately.

His jaw is clenched, and I know that I'm in trouble. "I'm sorry, Springer. I don't know what came over me. Seeing him grabbed like that...I just lost it."

He lets out an exasperated breath. "Enora, you have to watch what you say and do around these people. I can't believe you punched her. What you did was careless and dangerous."

"I know. I'm sorry. I just saw him being grabbed and couldn't stop myself."

"Look, I calmed everyone down and told them you're really protective of the boy because he's such a valuable asset. But I can tell you that not all of them bought it, and some of them are going to be gunning for you."

I look away, irritated that he apologized for me. "I didn't mean to offend anyone, but what the hell was I supposed to do? Just let them toss him around like he's something they can use?"

Springer shakes his head slowly. "That's not what I'm implying. You threatened them, Enora, and that was a mistake."

I look down, feeling ashamed that I let my anger take over because I know he's right. "How do I fix it?"

"You can't. That woman you punched? Her name is Piper. Her cousin was the kid who died in your arms at the food processing plant." It feels like a punch in the gut when he says this. "Yeah. I can't even address that issue. Look, you need to know that she's got a small crew that left the room with her after issuing threats. I won't have any sway over how that pans out."

"Crap. I didn't think, okay? I just reacted."

"I know, and I understand. Honestly, I was pretty close

to doing the same thing. Let's just try to lay low for a bit. Okay, slugger?"

"I'll try." And I want to, but I also know that I can't make any promises. The dark confines of this strange home begin to constrict.

CHAPTER FIFTEEN

The broadcast has the desired effect. Bands of people attack everything from Sentinels to supply depots. As all of this goes on, the DMC launches a media campaign to attack the resistance and lay blame at our feet. According to the DMC, rebels launched the attack on the peaceful protestors, slaughtering hundreds of innocent people. It is a powerfully frightening counterattack. Following this, broadcasts from General Malvolia are interspersed during regular programming throughout the day. There is footage of rebels attacking food production plants and citizens in their communications, though I have to wonder how much of this is real.

To counter this, rebels in various divisions try to hack into broadcasts to show their own clips, adding fuel to the movement. But the worry is growing. The DMC has inexhaustible resources and power. Ours is severely limited.

Springer sees this as our opportunity. During a briefing with Sergeant Quinn, Springer and I are given an analysis of how the Company has begun to slow or stop the supply chain in retaliation for uprisings. These interruptions have been blamed on the resistance through General Malvolia's communications. Until now, the few locations of greatest resistance have been able to subsist on the resources already within the town limits, but those are dwindling quickly, some having been inadvertently destroyed during the initial fighting. Now the tables are turning, in the Company's favor, as people are becoming desperate.

"Unless we can coordinate an effort to access and distribute food and water to our troops so we can send help to the people in these towns, this movement will die before it's truly begun." Sergeant Quinn pulls up a map of the supply depots closest to us. Less than a handful of locations successfully took control of their community, leaving our efforts to support the towns very minimal. It's disheartening, and I'm not sure if it's a relief or frustration that Prineville is not on the list. Of those towns that originally made a stand, most fell under the power of the DMC. "We are looking at a coordinated attack on two major facilities in our part of the state. If we can successfully complete a large-scale raid, then supplies can be distributed to our different divisions and any surplus to those communities fighting with us."

This is exactly what I knew would happen once all

this began. Without food and water, rebels and civilians would surrender. There is just no way to stay in the fight when you have people crying in hunger. I walk over to the map and find our current location. We could easily get to one of the facilities, and I know the system inside and out.

And then a new thought pops into my head. "Why hasn't the DMC bombed these uprisings?"

Sergeant Quinn looks at me with strangely cold eyes. "I don't know."

I glance at Springer, but he turns his face away. Is he hiding something from me? I begin to worry about my parents. Has Prineville been attacked, and he just doesn't want me to know? My heart aches at the thought, and I feel my mind start to unravel. I want to ask Springer what he knows but am stopped from voicing my question when there is a knock at the door, and a man talks briefly with Sergeant Quinn. I don't see who he is, but I notice that he passes a flash drive to the sergeant. When she closes the door, she turns to me with a grave expression.

"What is it?" I ask. "Has Prineville been attacked?"

"You've been sent a message. This came through from another division and was passed along to us." She quickly installs and uploads a video.

I gasp when Drake's face fills the screen. "Hello, Enora. I have a message for you. Please watch and listen."

The video pans right.

"Enora." It's my mother speaking, her voice clear and reproachful, but there is something off about it all. The moment I see it, my heart starts racing. My parent's arms are pulled behind their backs as though cuffed. I can see faint bruising on my mother's wrinkled cheek while my father looks emaciated. Her voice continues as I accept that my parents have been arrested and tortured. "You need to surrender. What you've done is very wrong. You've endangered everyone's life with your actions. The DMC is here to keep us safe, and you've turned into a traitor. We were told that you've stolen things. It's time for you to leave these rebels. They are not your friends. They are the enemy. Please stop what you're doing. This isn't who you are."

There must have been some signal behind the camera because it's suddenly my father talking. "Listen to your mother, Enora. You must stop this madness." My father looks so old and frail, like all of this has added ten years to his face. It's heart-wrenching to see and hear them. "These groups of traitors you're with are using you. They are hurting people. You need to do the right thing and surrender." I don't have more than a few seconds to think about what they said and what it could mean because Drake's face reappears.

"That doesn't even faze you, does it? You're not going to listen. In fact, I bet you don't even care about them. So, I'll make this easier for you, for all of us. No point in wasting water on these two anymore."

He sighs dramatically then bends his arm as though reaching for something. When I see what it is, I cry out. I watch in horror as he cocks a gun and turns to my parents.

"No! Oh, God! No!" I scream over the harsh sobs and begging of my parents. He shoots my mother first, a bullet piercing her between the eyes, violently throwing her head backward. My father is sobbing her name, not even looking as Drake aims the gun to his temple and fires.

Springer is holding me in a tight embrace as I fall apart, screaming and crying. Drake turns to the camera.

"You did this. Just remember that. None of this would've happened if not for you. Goodbye, Enora." The video goes black, and all that can be heard are my hoarse sobs.

Sergeant Quinn steps out of the room. I collapse on the floor in Springer's lap. "I killed them. I killed my parents."

"No."

"Yes, I did. You heard him."

"You didn't pull the trigger, Enora."

"They looked so scared. It's my fault. It's all my fault."

Springer turns me to face him. "Don't you do that! Don't let that bastard get into your head and twist the truth. You didn't give the order to kill your parents. You didn't pull that trigger. That was General Malvolia's deci-sion. Drake was just her puppet."

I cry for a while longer as Springer whispers comforting things in my ear. Eventually, the tears stop. There's just not enough moisture in my body to even make them anymore. My chest hurts from my shuddered breaths, and I lean into Springer, resting my head against his chest.

"You're all I have left." It hurts to say that, to know the truth of it. He's all there is that can tie me to this life.

"I'll never leave you, Enora."

I know he means it, but there are some promises none of us can make. When I'm calm enough, Springer gets up and steps out of the room to speak with Sergeant Quinn. I stay on the floor, too drained to do anything but sit there and try to come to terms with what I saw happen.

My parents are gone. In my heart, I knew the Company would use them against me. I had just held out hope that maybe they would be shown mercy. It was a naïve wish. There is no mercy in this withered world.

An hour later, Sergeant Quinn returns to the room. Springer and I have moved to a couple of the uncomfortable chairs, having spent the time talking quietly, reminiscing about the happy memories I have. I push the sorrow deep into my mind, where I cannot feel it. I will face it later in quiet moments, but not now. I shore up my strength with promises of vengeance and look at the sergeant.

Determined to show the sergeant that I am an asset to the resistance, I offer to use the skills the DMC spent so much time developing during our training. "Sergeant, as you know, our last assignment as Pathfinder and Sweeper was at one of these locations. I think Springer and I could assist you." I feel Springer unobtrusively squeeze my fingers as I talk. His presence helps me focus.

Sergeant Quinn considers my suggestion, and I'm relieved when she says, "Your assistance would be very beneficial. I would like you to have either Farrel or Corin join you. They can be monitoring the premises while you focus on infiltrating the security systems."

"I would like to have both of them with me. Corin has shown a stronger aptitude for the mapping systems, and Farrel is very successful with surveillance equipment."

"That would be fine."

Springer jumps into the conversation, eager to be part of the attack. "How soon would you like us to be ready?"

The sergeant looks over at him. "Anxious for some action?" She laughs at his expression and adds. "Well, I suppose you and Enora aren't used to being holed up like caged rats. All right, I would like you to be prepared to leave tomorrow night."

We spend the remainder of the day, and the next, going over logistics together and then with our trainees. I try not to dwell on the fact that I am able to go on, that thoughts of my parents stay in the peripheral and don't overwhelm me. Perhaps I am becoming too jaded by this life.

Farrel and Corin are incredibly excited when I announce their involvement. I worry about them being too young to understand the risks of attacking a DMC facility, but there's nothing I can do about their immaturity. I can only hope I don't end up with their blood on my hands. As the two of them chatter excitedly, I wonder how Springer and Donovan are doing with their child soldiers. The one benefit they have is that the adults who've been focused on supply raids will be joining the troops. This should give us the numbers we need to be successful. I just hope we don't have many casualties, as this group of rebels is growing thin.

Hal is more than willing to look after Ander when we broach the subject later on. He's taken on the role of father to such a degree that I wonder if Ander would be better off with Hal full time. Of course, that's not a choice I can make, but Hal has the experience that Springer and I don't.

As Springer and I pack our gear, I am quiet, lost in thoughts of my parents. I refuse to let the grief overwhelm me as I picture their faces. Unbidden, Bram's image joins theirs as I sift through memories of childhood. I feel unanchored, having lost everyone I knew when I was young. But then I realize that maybe I didn't. Safa may still be alive, somewhere. I wonder if I could find her and if Springer and I could rescue her from Company control. I latch onto that thought as I finish packing my gear for the attack. Tonight, I will find a way to hack into the DMC database and find her.

. . .

We leave the compound at one in the morning, using electric jeeps to transport our fighters to a vast sewer system, a relic of the past, which will enable us to get as close to the food processing facility as possible before hoofing it the rest of the way. The mood is positive, though muted by the events that have spread like fire through our division, as we hop out of the jeeps and head below ground. By now, everyone has heard about the death of my family. I've received numerous sorrowful looks and condolences, but I've hardened my feelings, unwilling to let myself fall apart.

It takes a half-hour trekking through the dark sewer to get to our exit point, a position that is still a short hike to the plant. Springer splits up our contingent of soldiers, and we make our way to the outskirts of the food processing facility in small groups. While this is not the location that Springer and I had been previously assigned to, I know that all of these plants are constructed similarly and use this information to conduct our attack.

Once we get to the stopping point outside the perimeter, Springer and I get out our gear, and I open up my computer. Hacking into the system is fairly straightforward, but I note that there are a few new security measures. A less careful person may have missed these, but I was looking for anything unusual, having assumed that the Company would have increased security after the uprisings began.

I let Springer know when we are ready, and he slinks

closer to the guard tower in the northern corner of the plant. I stay behind with five others in our small unit, waiting for the all-clear before breaking into the airshafts. I ruthlessly shut out the memory of another one of these groups entering a similar facility and my part in the tragic ending of that effort. Training my scope to follow Springer's movements, I watch the red glow of a guard fall over the side of the tower and hear a muffled thump when he hits the ground. The body is still. That's one.

There are no other guards in the tower, so I indicate that we proceed. Farrel and Corin station themselves in a location that allows them to see the bulk of the grounds surrounding the plant. I've instructed them to stay out of sight and let the soldiers do the fighting. I hope they listen.

Needing to get inside the building so I can hack directly into the system, Springer and I move forward with our small group of fighters. I'm thankful Springer has chosen only adults to join us, leaving Donovan with the larger contingent of soldiers, most of them young and inexperienced. One of our crew cuts through the fence as Springer joins us. We make our way to a ventilation shaft, and in minutes we're in.

It's a claustrophobic feeling as we head deeper into the ducts. I work to keep my breathing quiet as we move along. Finally, we reach a food storage room, the least risky location and centrally located for access to the heart of the facility. Springer positions himself above the vent and carefully pulls it off, sliding it onto the opposite side of the duct. I use the scope to do a quick scan, but nothing is living in there. Carefully, we lower ourselves into the room and head to the door. From here, we'll be separating. It's up to Springer and me to get to the main computer. Once I've shut everything down, completely disconnecting this place from the Company's watchful eye, we will alert the second wave of fighters and attack.

I quickly create a loop in the remote security feed to leave the room unnoticed. "Let's go."

Springer and I make our way through the corridors. I can see from his expression that he's totally in his element, alert and virtually humming with excitement. It's a relief when we make it to a room that looks strikingly similar to the one from our last DMC assignment. I put my gear down and pull a chair up to the computer. Springer remains at the door, keeping guard.

Hacking into the system takes me a bit longer than it should, and I start to sweat, thinking maybe I won't be able to pull this off. But eventually, I find a backdoor, and I'm in. I use this as a means to exploit the network. Unbeknownst to Springer, I'm also looking for Safa. I need to know where she is, if she is alive. I begin the search and soon find a few files that reference her name. Only one of them indicates Prineville as her location. The others are DMC facilities.

"What's taking so long?" Springer's voice is impatient.

I shake my head and wave his question away, having

just found a file of current status. Springer walks over to me, curious. "What the hell are you doing?"

"Ssh. Just give me a minute."

"Enora, we could be found out at any minute. This is not the time to go digging through the system. You're putting us all at risk!" He reaches over as though to push my hands aside, but it's too late. I've found what I've been looking for, and it's shocked me.

"Oh my God." I scoot the chair back and stand up, pointing to the screen. Springer looks at it for a few moments, then turns back to me.

"Who's Safa?"

"Remember, she's my friend, my best friend, from back home. The day I left, she was arrested, and I've wondered, all this time, what happened to her."

"Okay. So what happened?"

"She's *here.*"

CHAPTER SIXTEEN

I am stunned. At once, desperate to find her, while afraid of what I will see when I do.

"You mean your friend, Safa, is here? In this facility?" Springer sounds incredulous. I look at him. My eyes must appear as frantic as I feel because he reaches over to calm me down. "Hey, are you okay?"

"I wanted to find her, but I never...I didn't think I really would. We have to get her out of here!"

Springer holds up his hands. "Wait. Are you serious? Enora, we can't do that. This whole thing is risky enough. If we take her with us, they'll use her tracer to track her, and when they do, they'll find us!" I shake my head, unwilling to budge. "Do you think the Company doesn't know her connection to you? The moment they become aware of our attack, our names and anyone we knew, will be first on the list to track. You could end up killing us all! Do you want that blood on your hands?"

I hear him, and I get it, but I have to do this. All I see is that moment when her body was slammed against the ground while I just looked on in horror. And then I left her behind. Just like I left my parents behind to be butchered. "I have to, Springer. I can't leave her again. I can't lose anyone else."

He's frustrated with me, pinching the bridge of his nose, thinking of what to say to sway me. "Enora, what if the person you knew is gone?"

I can't think that. I owe Safa. "I don't care. I need to find her."

"We could all end up dead because of this."

"I won't let it come to that." He turns his back to me, and I reach out and gently grasp his shoulder, trying to turn him to face me. "What if it were *you*? Do you think I could just leave you behind?"

"I would expect you to."

There is a hard glint in his eyes. He means what he says. If he were captured or injured, he would want me to leave and save myself. But I couldn't do that, and I'm not going to do that now. "No."

I watch his scowl deepen, while behind his eyes, I see him planning how to stop me. "We need to focus on why we're here." I just look at him. "Enora, you need to look beyond this. We have a job to do."

"Fine."

I can see that he doesn't buy my easy surrender, but there's no time to argue. I turn back to the screen and spend a few minutes severing the connection with the Company. Our time will be limited at this point as there are numerous fail-safes that are sure to kick in and override what I've done. If we don't have complete control over this building by the Company's alerted, we'll have to abandon our efforts and run.

As soon as I've finished, I turn to Springer. "Alert the second team." This action will bring the bulk of our fighters, though that term is hardly accurate considering the ages and abilities. They simply don't have the experience or know-how that we do, and I have little faith that we'll be able to make a stand for long.

I listen as Springer gives the command and watch the security feed from the perimeter of the building. It doesn't take long before the fighting begins, and it quickly becomes apparent that not all of the people on our side have the stomach for it. I watch, as though outside myself, as one twenty-something woman points her gun at a guard who is charging toward her but is unable to pull her trigger. The force of a bullet strikes her chest, propelling her body backward. I watch as the guard tramples her twitching form while aiming for the next target. Three bodies later, Springer is out the door, racing to the scene. I know I should stay and watch, make sure he's safe. But this is my opportunity to find Safa.

The data I pulled up indicated that she is working as

an assistant in a hydroculture unit. If that's what it sounds like, I'm happy she ended up here instead of in a role like mine. All she ever wanted was to tinker with her many experiments, and that last one she dabbled in had to do with a simple system to grow plants. Having determined where that unit is housed, I begin to make my way there, keeping to the nooks and shadows when I can. At any moment, I know all hell is going to break loose.

I'm halfway there when I hear the distinct popping sound of gunfire from within the compound. Picking up my pace, I sprint down the halls, heedless of everyone in my desperate attempt to get to Safa. But other sounds are coming closer, shouts and running feet, and time has run out. In front of me, a door bursts open, releasing a horde of Sentinels who take one look at me and begin firing. The first slug grazes my left shoulder, making me lose my footing and crash into the wall. The second hits my thigh with a sickening thud, and I collapse.

I don't feel any pain, which seems strange. There is just numbness and ringing in my ears. I'm lying on my side, face to the wall. I can feel the vibrations of feet thumping against the cold tiles as Sentinels run past me. Keeping still, I pretend to be dead. I feel a hard kick in my back as one man investigates whether or not I'm alive. Biting my inner cheek, I don't make a sound, and he continues on.

Ultimately, the pain comes, and I have to smother a scream as I take it in. I wriggle onto my back and fumble

with my belt, tugging it free of my waist to use as a tourniquet. The blood makes my hands slippery, and I'm beginning to panic as minutes pass, and I still haven't been able
to bind my leg. A sob bursts from my mouth as I imagine
myself bleeding out on this floor, far from Springer.

It takes a moment to realize that I am not alone. Next
to me is a pair of standard-issue, black boots. Just like the
ones I was given on the day I graduated. I follow the soles
of the shoes up dark slacks and shirt, past the hard stumble
on a firm chin, and into eyes that hold no compassion. I
never thought I would have to see his face again. I remember, all too clearly, the snide comments and disdain that
dripped from every look and action back during my training. Drake told me he'd been reassigned from my unit and
sent off to a production plant. It makes perfect sense that
he'd be a Sentinel, one of those vicious drones who wield
their flimsy power over the weak and ordinary.

"Well, well, well. Look at what we have here." Nero's
voice sneers. He crouches down, resting his arms on his
knee. "It's Enora, right?"

I can't speak, my voice having frozen along with my
heart.

"I remember you. You're that pleb who thought she
was hot-shit." He shakes his head and runs his tongue
along his lower lip. "Not so hot now."

He reaches over, squeezing my leg at the site of the
bullet hole. I feel my body begin to spasm, whether from
fear or pain. I unlock my jaw and scream, neck arching.

He chuckles. "I should put a bullet in your head, but you know what? I wouldn't want to waste one on you." Another scream rips from my chest as he squeezes my leg again before standing up.

I am panting in pain and terror as I look into merciless eyes towering over me. I know he's going to hurt me, and I don't think I can take it. "Here's a little souvenir to remember me by, not that you'll live much longer, but I wouldn't want you to forget me, pleb." I watch, unable to move, as he lifts his leg to bring it down on my thigh. I clench my eyes, trying to prepare myself, but knowing I can't.

I hear a strange sound, followed by the muted smack of a body hitting the floor. Slowly, I open my eyes and turn my head. A yelp escapes as I come face to face with Nero's vacant stare. Blood is pooling on the floor behind his head, and he's motionless. I can't look away. His dead eyes have me trapped as though I'm tethered. I can't make sense of it.

And then I feel hands softly shaking my body and hear a voice I never thought to hear again. "Enora?"

CHAPTER SEVENTEEN

Safa is crouched next to me, tugging my belt into place to staunch the flow of blood from my bullet wound. I still haven't said a word, my voice gone as my mind tries to piece together how she's here. She looks so different. Her hair is shorn, leaving a short layer around her head. The face I remember so well is hard now, with lines of defeat etched into the curves around her mouth. She's pale and worn, though I can see that it's not from lack of food. Instead, it's as though her youth has been sucked out of her, leaving a shell of who she was.

I glance at Nero's body. The blood has stopped flowing, and he's just lying there, dead. I can see a club, stained red, resting on the floor, about a foot away. How did she even know I was here?

I clear my throat and try to speak, but it comes out cracked and indecipherable. Forcing myself to swallow what little spit sits in my mouth, I cough to clear my throat and try again. "Safa?"

She gives one more tug to secure the tourniquet before answering. "I'm here, Enora."

"How?" I ask. There are so many layers to the simple question. How did she get through arrest and its inevitable consequences? How did she get recruited? How did she end up in this place? How did she know I was here and needed help? It is the last thought that gives me pause.

I see her face smile down at me, it's the same smile, but it looks all wrong. It's as though she's mimicking some former part of herself. It doesn't reach her eyes, and it doesn't reflect her spirit. "It's a long story, too long for me to tell now. I need to get you out of here before someone finds us."

As she reaches over to lift me into a sitting position, I bat her hand away. "I need to know, now. How did you know I was here?"

"I didn't. I heard the noises and was heading toward the sounds of fighting. I had a feeling it was a group of rebels, and I wanted to help. Then I found you, with Nero. I'm sorry I couldn't stop him sooner. I was just so shocked to look around the corner and see you, with him crouched over you. I thought my mind was playing tricks on me."

I look closely at her face as she speaks, trying to decide if it's really her. She's so changed from the girl I remember. There's a hardness now and something else I can't put my finger on. "It's okay. The worst of the damage had already been done. He was just going to make it a lot more painful." She nods, her mouth pinching as she takes in my wounds. "Safa, how is it that you're *here*, in this place?"

She lets out a long sigh before standing up and moving behind me. I feel her hands slip under my arms, and then she begins to drag me away from the sounds of battle and into the hall she had come from. As Safa pulls me through the passages to someplace she feels is safe, she tells me her story. "I don't know who turned me in. It could've been a few people, honestly. For a while, I even thought it might have been you."

I gasp at this. "Me? Safa, I would never do that! How could you even think it?"

She shakes her head while dragging me the last few feet into a small room with a bed. I watch as she pulls the door closed and then hoists me onto the hard mattress. I let out a breath of relief when my head hits the pillow. Outside the room, we hear the fighting continue, gunshots ringing out. I hope that leaving my post hasn't doomed us all.

I feel weak and sick to my stomach. Focusing on taking deep breaths, I try to calm the nausea. Safa sits on the edge, looking blankly at the wall trwhile I compose myself.

"You were so different after your recruitment, always hanging out with the drones. When I was interrogated after the arrest, I blamed you. I thought they had completely changed you, made you into one of them."

"Oh, Safa. I could never do that."

She nods, dropping her chin. "I know, in my heart, I knew." She stands and digs through the upper drawer of a small dresser, pulling out a white undershirt. I watch as she leans over me and unbuttons my blouse to see the wound on my shoulder. It hurts when she presses the fabric against it. "The interrogation lasted for hours, maybe days. It felt like days. When they were done with me, I had told them everything. They broke my teeth. Did you know that? I couldn't even be questioned until they had capped them, and I could use my mouth again. And then, one day, I saw you in the announcements. They called you a water traitor. It made me so happy to see you up there."

I wince as she lifts the fabric off my shoulder. "This one isn't bad. It looks like it just grazed you." I see her face turn toward my leg, and she frowns. "The leg is much worse. We need to get you out of here."

"It can wait, just a little longer."

I watch emotions flash across her face as she considers whether or not to let me have my way. "Enora, you need to get medical help. Are there any doctors with the rebels?"

"No. Don't worry about me right now. We'll deal with that soon enough. Just tell me first. Tell me how you got to this place." I know that if Springer finds me, he'll haul me out of here and leave Safa behind unless I can somehow convince him to take her with us. But there's no way I can do that unless I know the truth.

"I don't know how long I spent in confinement after being questioned. It was probably only a couple of weeks. I was asked repeatedly about my associations and eventually about the garden itself during that time. They actually brought it in, and some man I hadn't seen before asked me to explain the design."

"Is that why you ended up here?"

"Yeah. While I hadn't invented anything new by their standards, I guess one of the scientists thought I'd be useful here and requested my relocation to this facility." Safa stops, looking down at her hands, now smeared with my blood. "I was so sure they were going to kill me. My parents must think I'm dead."

I'm slightly appalled by this news. "They've never let you call them?"

She shakes her head. "I'm not really a Company employee, Enora."

"They killed my parents."

"Oh, Enora! I'm so sorry."

I gulp, remembering the images branded in my mind forever. "They shot them in the head. There was a video. It was a warning."

She squeezes my hand. "I'm so sorry."

"That's why I needed to look for you. I have no one left from my life before all of this. I wanted to find you. I needed to find you."

Safa looks at me, and the hardness in her gaze grows soft. "I never thought I'd see you again. When your name and face showed up in so many newscasts, I thought you'd stay hidden or try to get far away from here."

"I'm here to fight the Company any way I can. But someday, I hope to be free."

"Yeah. I used to hope for that too." She looks so empty when she says this.

"What do you mean?"

Safa's eyes meet mine with such defeat. "I'm a slave."

"I don't understand."

"I'm not like how you were when you were recruited. I don't get any special privileges and never will. They've made that very clear." As she talks, Safa takes another look at my leg to make sure the blood hasn't started flowing again. "There's never going to be any more than what I am now. I'll never get out of here."

I reach over and grab her hand. "Yes, you will. I'm going to get you out. You can join us and fight all of this."

"Oh, Enora. I wish I could."

"You can!"

Her eyes look dead, empty of any hope. It's heartbreaking to see. "No. I will never leave this place. One step beyond the gates, and I'll be killed."

"What? I don't know what you're saying." Safa leans back, swinging up her right leg, and pulls aside the cuff of her pant. Around her ankle is a type of bracelet, one I have never seen before. "What the hell is *that*?"

"Their guarantee that I can't escape." When I just stare at it, she continues. "There are sensors throughout the band that have tiny triggers. If I leave the compound without the device having been disengaged, it'll stop my heart with a bolt of electric current and then send out an alert to the Company."

I sink into the mattress as she says this, unable to stop the hopeless feeling from passing through my brain. "That's barbaric."

She nods. "But effective. So, you see, I can't go with you."

"Maybe we can find a way to reprogram it. You know, a tech guru modified the signal in my microchip. I'm sure she could do something for you."

"How?"

"Springer could help. He's out there fighting. If we get to him, he could somehow get word to our sergeant, and we could get you out."

"Who's Springer?"

"He's my partner, my Sweeper, before all of this." Safa looks unsure as I say this. "He's on our side, Safa. Bram trusted him and arranged it all."

"Bram?'

There's no time to explain everything. That'll have to keep. "I can't get into that now. Just know that you can trust Springer."

"Okay." Her eyes sweep over me. "You're in no shape to go anywhere, though."

"With your help, I could. He's our only hope to get you out of here."

Leaning heavily on Safa, I limp out of the room with her, and we slowly make our way toward the sound of yelling and gunfire. Sweat pops out across my forehead, and I begin to feel faint and nauseous, my leg throbbing. Safa can sense my discomfort, and she helps me to lower myself to the floor, resting my back against the wall. The cool surface feels good, and I concentrate on breathing deeply to overcome the urge to vomit. We are so close to the fighting that as I sit there, I can hear the awful sounds of bullets meeting flesh, that horrible thunk which is so different than when they rip through walls or objects. I wonder how many of our fighters have fallen.

"Enora, what does he look like?"

"It's too hard for me to describe him. He'll just look like all the others to you. Help me up."

We finally make it to a corridor just beyond the fringes of the combat. Safa pokes her head around the corner and then pulls me over. I take a quick look, shying away from the bodies crumpled on the floor. I don't see him right away, as his back is to me. He's crouched behind some kind of barrier, looking for targets. I point him out to Safa. She nods and pushes me gently against the wall so that I can lean against it for support. Dropping low to the ground, she darts toward Springer, somehow avoiding his notice and anyone else's. I sigh in relief when she maneuvers herself next to him. From my vantage point, I can see her mouth forming his name and watch as he jumps to the side, startled, and then focuses on her. Safa says something and points to me. The look on Springer's face is one of profound relief. I sag against the wall, the tension that's been building leaving my muscles as the pain returns.

Springer pushes Safa in front of him, and they quickly make their way to me. The moment Springer is close enough, he drops to his knees and grabs my shoulders. "Dammit, Enora! I told you to stay where you were."

"I know."

"You're going to give me gray hair. What the hell did you do to yourself?" He begins probing my injuries.

"Ouch!"

He shakes his head. "You could've been killed."

"But I wasn't."

He takes a look at the tourniquet, nodding to himself when he sees that it's working well. "So, this is Safa, huh?"

"Yeah. If not for her, I'd be dead."

"If not for your recklessness," he glowers. "You wouldn't have any injuries, to begin with."

"Springer..."

"I know. I know. So, what's the plan?"

I explain the issue with the ankle bracelet and watch Springer contemplate that problem. He knows that I don't want to leave Safa behind. I can see him calculating the risks of trying to get her out of here. "I don't know how to get that off or reprogram it. Maybe Sergeant Quinn has an idea of what we can do, or we could question one of the Sentinels we've captured. You're lucky leaving your post didn't doom this whole operation. If not for those two kids you trained, we would've been taken by surprise and overrun when a group of Sentinels tried to flank us."

"I'm sorry, Springer. I had to do it."

"I guess I can forgive you, but I'm not sure that Sergeant Quinn will. Look, whatever we need to do, let's do it. We may be winning this little battle now, but it's not going to take long for reinforcements to arrive."

Springer pauses and looks over at Safa, who averts her eyes. "Enora, you have to understand that the likelihood of us being able to get her out is slim at best. If Sergeant Quinn isn't willing to risk it, then we'll have no choice."

I know what he's saying, but I can't accept the possibility that I may have to leave Safa behind again. "We have to try."

"Okay. Let's go." Springer hauls me up, careful not to jostle me, and we head toward an exit away from the majority of the fighting.

Safa walks behind us, keeping watch for anyone who may come from that direction. Eventually, we get to a hallway that will lead us outside the building. Springer tells us to wait while he jogs ahead to scout out the exit and ensure we won't get ambushed. It feels so good to sit down. My leg feels numb now, which is better than the pain, I suppose, but it's making it harder for me to walk.

Safa crouches down in front of me. "How are you holding up?"

"As good as can be expected, I guess."

Springer begins to jog back to us, and I watch, brow

crinkling, as he suddenly stretches out a hand as though to ward something off and yells, "No!"

The sound of a gun fired close to my head makes me feel as though my ear imploded, the subsequent ringing confusing my mind. I feel my leg explode in pain as weight comes crashing down on me. I look at my lap, mouth gaping in bewilderment, trying to make sense of what I'm seeing. Is that Safa? I can't make out her features. The entire right side of her face is gone, replaced by a bloody pulp. Her body twitches against my legs.

I don't know when I begin screaming, my hands pressing against the rush of blood pouring from the wound in a desperate attempt to staunch the flow.

"No...no...no!" The bleeding won't stop, and I can feel her life slipping away. "Safa!" I sob though I know it's too little, too late.

"Safa – please don't leave me." Beneath a mess of gore, I see one eye is open, but there's nothing there, no recognition, just a blank stare. "I'm sorry, Safa. I'm so sorry."

I dimly realize that Springer is yelling at someone, but I can't make out what he's saying. All I can do is look in horror as Safa's life bleeds out of her. Tears stream, unchecked, down my cheeks, making lines in the blood splatter. Safa's body goes still, and though I can't hear it beyond the ringing in my ears, I see her last breath.

Springer drops to his knees next to me and places his fingers along Safa's neck. I know he'll find no pulse. She's gone. I couldn't save her. In the fringes of my mind, I can feel the weight of this realization waiting to crash over me.

"What happened?"

Springer says something, but it's hard for me to make it out. He jerks his head toward someone I didn't realize was there, standing a few feet away. I turn my head and look into a vaguely familiar face. I watch the sneer creep over her features, and that's when it clicks. Piper. The woman I punched in the face.

"You can thank me later," she smirks.

I try to lunge at her, but Safa's weight and my leg prevent me from moving. "*Why?* She was my friend, you hateful bitch!"

"If she was your friend, then you're a traitor." With that, Piper saunters away.

The gunfire has ceased. Our forces take control of the compound and confiscate as many supplies as possible before returning to our headquarters. We have won.

I'm unable to gather the energy or motivation to move. The grief is crushing. My strength is fading, and my will to muster it is gone. What is all of this for? The Company murdered my best friend and family. Now, rebels have killed Safa. How is any of this right? Who are the 'good guys' in all of this?

"Enora." Springer's voice is laced with worry. "Let's get you out of here." He picks me up and cradles me to his chest. There are bodies everywhere as we make our way out of the building, some ours but most theirs. Springer picks his way through the melee, trying his best not to bump me. My hands feel sticky. I look down at them and see the layer of blood and brain matter caked across my palms and between my fingers. I stare at it, unable to do anything more.

"Safa," I whisper.

Springer looks down at me. "I'm sorry, Enora."

My voice breaks. "Safa."

I let him carry me on, past the evidence of our infiltration and the macabre scenes of death. Safa is gone, and once again, I am leaving her behind.

The guard towers are now manned with rebels as Springer carries me away from the carnage. Just inside the perimeter of the fence is a line of Sentinels, on their knees with hands behind their necks. The eyes of all but a couple are downcast. Those brave few that glare at our forces find themselves with guns pointed in their faces. I wonder if they will be rash enough to put up a fight. Even if they don't, I already know the conclusion to this night's work. We have no resources to support captives. Thankfully, Springer and I are able to leave the premises entirely before I have to watch the inevitable outcome. But I can still hear the popping sound.

CHAPTER EIGHTEEN

I have no memory of returning to the underground compound, having passed out from pain and blood loss somewhere along the way. Springer is nowhere to be seen when I come to, and I find myself in Dr. Kane's care. I steel myself against her glare as she checks my bandages.

"You're fortunate to be alive." I don't reply, only look at her questioningly.

She indicates my leg. "Another couple inches over, and the bullet would've severed an artery. You would've bled to death in minutes."

I shift my focus to my leg and gingerly move it, testing my pain tolerance and stiffness. "Can I walk on it?" I just want to get out of here, away from her oily presence.

"As long as you take it slowly, that should be fine. Don't get careless and tear the stitches open."

I nod and ask, "What have you heard about the raid?"

"I heard that you abandoned your post and put our forces at risk. If it were up to me, I'd have you hung." Her smirk is meant to push my buttons.

I want to snap at her, but I resist the urge. There's no argument I could give. She's right. I departed my post. I was reckless and left the people I was meant to protect to their fate to save my friend. In the end, those actions killed her. This cold woman wouldn't understand the bonds of friendship that drove me to my choice.

She looks mildly disappointed at having been robbed of an opportunity to further put me in my place as I just stare at her in silence. I slowly sit up, fighting off a wave of dizziness at the movement. Kane ignores me, all too happy to let me struggle as I stand, wincing in pain as my leg muscles pull on the injury.

I hobble out the door, using the walls for support, and slowly make my way to my quarters. A film of sweat has covered my face, and my whole body is shaking with exertion by the time I finally make it. I push the door open, expecting to find Springer, or at least Hal with Ander, but the space is empty. I make my way to my bed and lower myself face down onto the mattress. My body aches, and I feel queasy as I lie there. There's a good chance I did some harm to my healing process by leaving Kane's office, but I couldn't stand to be there any longer.

The next thing I know, Springer is gently shaking me. "No..." I mumble, trying to pull away from him.

"Enora, you need to wake up."

I open my eyes slowly and start to shift my body. "Oh ow, that hurts." I groan as I roll over. Springer sits on the edge of the mattress, waiting for me to come fully awake.

"Hey," I finally manage to choke out.

His eyes crinkle a little, but the smile doesn't reach his mouth. "How are you feeling?"

"Sore. Tired." I leave out the deeper feelings, the loss, and the anger. They're just too fresh.

"Yeah, I figured you would be. Glad you got some rest." I can see that there's something he wants to say, but he bites his tongue, respecting my need to keep some things inside until I'm ready.

I appreciate his acceptance and switch to a topic I can discuss. "What's the news?"

He sighs and shifts his body so that his elbows rest on his knees. He looks defeated. "Our raid was one of a handful that was successful, and on the largest scale. Never before has a division been able to gain control of a DMC facility for such an extended period of time. And the amount of supplies we collected is enormous compared to previous raids. However, if resistance forces are unable to get supplies on a larger scale elsewhere, how can we sustain this fight?"

"We can't," I reply softly, though I know Springer wasn't looking for an answer.

The simple truth is that the Company has all the power because they have all the resources. If the people who rise up in towns and cities across the country have no access to food or water, the Company will simply starve them out. It wouldn't take long. And by the time the last opposition fell, those who remained would be a defeated lot, ready to accept anything just to survive.

This all feels like a losing battle. Bram is gone. My parents were murdered. Safa's dead. The resistance is holding on by a thread, and I'm not sure who they really are anymore. What is it all for if people don't care about each other? How many more have to die? My heart aches, and I feel lost.

"Where's Ander?"

"He's with Hal. They came by while you were asleep but left so you could rest."

"What are they going to do with him?"

"Right now, nothing, at least as far as I've been told." But I can see that he's bothered by something. I'm tempted to push him about it to find out what he thinks Sergeant Quinn may have planned, but my eyes are getting droopy, and it feels like too much effort to ask. So I let it go. He'll talk to me when he's ready. For now, I need to heal and sleep. And try to forget.

A few minutes after I close my eyes, I feel Springer's weight lift from the bed. He leans over me and tucks strands of hair behind my ears, just like Bram used to. It fills me with a wave of sadness. I roll away from him, folding my arms to my chest in a futile effort to protect myself from the pain.

He lets out a slow breath, and I hear him straighten. "I'll be back to get you at dinner."

"Okay," I whisper and listen to his soft steps as he leaves the room. I welcome the nothingness when it comes, eager to forget everything in sleep.

Ander is sitting on my bed when I come to a few hours later. He's a good kid, quiet and unobtrusive. I watch him in silence as he tinkers with some gadget Hal must have made for him. As I lie there, I think back on what Springer left unsaid earlier when I asked what would happen to Ander. I'm not naïve enough to think that Commander Guire doesn't have some agenda when it comes to the boy.

I watch Ander, this deviation from the natural law, and wonder what I would do if the commander had some nefarious purpose in mind, some action that would hurt this child. As I consider the possibility, I realize that I couldn't let something like that happen. It's not right. I can't become a mindless weapon. That's what the Company wanted me to be, and that is what I have fought so hard against. This group of rebels is no different if they see a living being as some expendable weapon, and I would be no different if I let them. I couldn't save my parents or Bram and Safa. But I can save Ander if it comes to it.

The consequences would be severe. I have never seen anything beyond a hardened soldier in the demeanor and words of the commander. If I were to stand up to him, in defense of Ander, I have no doubt that he would make me suffer for it. I don't believe he'd kill me or anything, but he is too intent on the goal of this whole resistance to let someone as insignificant as me stand in his way.

Ander must feel my eyes on him because he turns to me. "You woke up!"

"Yeah, sorry I slept so long."

"You talked in your sleep."

"I did?" I'm a little worried about what I may have said.

"You were saying lots of things, but they didn't make sense. You're funny when you sleep-talk!"

I smile, trying to make it look genuine, though I can only imagine that what I said was steeped in nightmares laced with violence and death. "Maybe I had a silly dream. Whatcha got there?"

Ander holds what looks like a plastic-covered bundle with wires sticking out of it in my face. I lean back a bit to bring it into focus. As I get a better look, I can see that it's some kind of old radio. "Does it work?"

He looks at the odd lump with a crestfallen expression only the young can truly master. "No, but Hal thinks he can find some parts and maybe make it work."

Ander's attention drifts back to the hunk of plastic, and I let my mind wander away from his fidgeting fingers. It's my fault that he's here, stuck in the bowels of this underground tomb, playing with a broken radio. My path doesn't seem as clear as it once did. There are too many complications now, too many things I never considered.

Or maybe I just didn't want to see them and accept my part in all of it. Now, I feel torn. I need people to see and understand what Ander represents. The Aurora mutation is not some random experiment. They have been meticulously bred for a purpose, and it is all tied to this world we live in.

I think back on conversations I've had with Ander. Those 'bad kids' are likely byproducts of his mutation. I know in my heart that those kids who exhibited the behaviors were exterminated, just like all the others in that tomb under Renascence. Once his mutation is perfected, the Company can move to breed a new generation of people. When this happens, I wonder if the rest of us will become an endangered species.

I keep my focus on this. I have to be strong. I must let go of what I cannot control and hold to what I can. The people I love may be dead, but there is more to be done, more that must come to light. But before all of this is over, there will be a reckoning.

CHAPTER NINETEEN

The following day, Springer helps me make my way through the maze of corridors to what I've begun to call the 'war room.' That's what it feels like, this place where plans are made and secret communications are sent. Springer finds it amusing, and I take a small amount of joy in making him crack a smile. My pace is slow as I limp along. It's irksome to have to rely on him for help, but I woke up so stiff that I could barely move.

Before we cross the threshold to where Commander Guire and Sergeant Quinn await us, Springer leans down and says, "Behave."

"Seriously?" I look at him and roll my eyes.

He raises his eyebrows. "I mean it, Enora. Just listen and try to hold your temper."

"What? Do you think I'm going to act like a five-year-old? Geez, Springer. I'm not stupid."

"That's not what I meant. Just be nice."

"Yes, sir." I punctuate my words with a brief salute, to which he just shakes his head in exasperation.

Conversation stops when I limp into the room. Sergeant Quinn looks grim, and the commander is devoid of any outward emotion. "Enora, take a seat."

"Thank you." It feels a little awkward to have everyone watching my painful progress. The quiet and stoic atmosphere sets off alarms of warning. Once I'm settled, I fold my hands in my lap and wait for the hammer to fall.

The commander motions for Sergeant Quinn to begin. She stands and directs our attention to the screen. Before us is a picture of the food processing plant that we raided. Smaller screens overlay this photo with other plants, and I can only hope these were successfully breached.

She clears her throat and points to the largest image. "After taking control of the facility, we were able to collect and transport all portable foodstuffs in addition to water. These have been housed in this facility and will be distributed among other divisions."

Sergeant Quinn pauses and then pulls up what looks like a series of communications. "As expected, your hack into the system was discovered by the DMC within a couple of hours of the initial attack. On the screen are communiqués that we were able to grab before they used encryption that we have yet to break."

I look up at the screen and begin reading. The first few communications are basic alerts, but as I continue, I see other messages that are internal documents between people in an intelligence branch of the Company. This is confirmed when I see General Malvolia's name.

As I read the last entry, I suck in a breath: *Pathfinder, Enora Byrnes, and Sweeper, Ethan Springer, are targets, location unknown. Within their possession is DMC property that must be recovered intact. Pathfinder is the priority target. Sweeper is expendable.*

I look at Springer, but he shakes his head almost imperceptibly. I return my attention to the screen. We'll discuss this later, in privacy.

"As you can see," the sergeant continues. "The DMC is well aware of your part in this attack, as well as the fact that you broke into Renascence and stole the child. By broadcasting this official order from the general herself, we can only assume that this information was meant for us to find."

She lets that sink in for a few moments. "The general's actions are purposeful. By allowing us to intercept this transmission, she seems to be stating that she knows your approximate whereabouts. This was an inevitable risk, but one we were willing to take. However, in light of this and other reasons, you have become a liability to this operation."

I feel like the floor has opened under me when she says this. A liability? What about our work making the theft of Ander and our raid successful? Is that just a load of worthless crap? My anger at being dumped from a cause I risked my life for fills my heart, and I begin to rise from my chair, ready to let loose with a string of profanity. But Springer reaches over, anchoring my arm to the chair.

"Sergeant, can you explain what you mean by a liability?"

I feel Commander Guire's stare and have to fight the urge to glare at him. "I'll take this one, Sergeant Quinn."

Springer and I turn to him, and I can see that he's hoping I'll lose control and lash out. It's the gloat simmering under the surface of his eyes that keeps me from yelling. Instead, I swallow hard, lean back in my chair, and wait for him to clarify.

"General Malvolia's reach is far and her resources inexhaustible. We knew that it was just a matter of time before you both were connected to a specific faction. This particular raid was more of a test. We needed to see if it was possible to disrupt security long enough to conduct an extended raid." He's watching me carefully, perhaps hoping for a reaction, but I keep my expression blank. "Our other, more essential purpose was to see what you would do in a situation like this. We needed to know where your loyalty lies."

Commander Guire looks pointedly at me. This was not where I anticipated this conversation to go. "Did you think it was accidental that you ended up *here* Enora, at this compound, so close to the same plant as your friend? What was her name? Sarah?"

I'm unable to raise my voice above a whisper. "Safa."

I look at his knowing smile and want to slap it off of his face. "Ah yes, Safa. Unusual name. Unusual girl, too. I have to admit that I didn't foresee the outcome for her, an unfortunate incident. Your actions, on the other hand, were only too predictable.

You see, Enora, in order for us to truly bring down the DMC, we need absolute loyalty to our cause. There can be no allegiance to friends or family who live under their control. That just makes you vulnerable. And that is not something I will tolerate. You made your loyalty clear when you abandoned your post and left our troops vulnerable to attack."

"I don't understand," I say, my voice cracking despite my effort to moderate it.

"General Malvolia will pursue you with every resource at her disposal. By stealing the child, a feat that I was quite astonished you could pull off, you have shown her that you are very dangerous. Your work at the plant has further cemented that perception, as you are also a risk in their effort to eliminate our resistance. She is giving us an option by sending that transmission. Either we hand you and the child over, or she will unleash hell."

Springer, quiet up until this moment, interjects. "Commander, I would imagine that the general has been eager to see our capture since Commander Williams' interrogation. Why does the raid make us any more of a target? Or, for that matter, a danger to you?"

"The danger is in her allegiance!" Commander Guire jerks his finger at me as his voice slowly rises. "It's in her willingness to put the entire operation at risk to try to save someone who would've exposed us all!"

Springer keeps his voice level as he replies. "Sir, Enora's parents were murdered recently, and Safa was the last person left from her life back home. She and Safa have known each other all their lives. I can assure you, having seen the girl risk her life to save her friend, that she was never a danger to this operation."

"You can guarantee that? Were you with Enora throughout the raid?"

I can hear the frustration in Springer's voice. "No, I was not with her the entire time. But if not for Safa's actions, Enora would've bled to death."

The commander nods slowly. "I understand your point and appreciate your insight. However, no one was with Enora throughout the raid. Therefore, we can't know what she told this girl or anyone else she may have come across."

"What are you saying? That Enora is a Company spy?" The anger in Springer's voice is impossible to ignore. I am too stunned by all of this to do anything but sit here and try to take it in. How has it come to this?

"They want her alive. We can assume that is because

she's an asset to them. Or, perhaps they simply mean to interrogate her to ascertain our location or discover more information regarding her ties to Commander Williams. Either way, we cannot allow it."

Springer sits back with a thump. I can feel him look at me, but I can't tear my eyes away from the Commander. My body feels numb. I've risked everything...*everything*! And now what's to become of me?

"You and Enora will be reassigned. We hope that we can keep your whereabouts unknown by relocating you both to different divisions. There is even talk of moving one or both of you to another state for your protection, though this poses some logistical problems and is a riskier option."

My head starts to spin. Are they going to separate us? I can't leave Springer. I can't do this without him. I feel my pulse accelerate as anxiety sets in. My hands grip the armrests of my chair as Commander Guire elaborates.

"Your expertise has been invaluable to our mission here, and that knowledge must be utilized in other branches of the resistance. You've shown us that conducting a sustained raid is possible, and this information must be shared with others. In this way, you will be aiding in our efforts on a much larger scale. I am also hopeful that, with your cooperation, your findings in Renascence can be confirmed in other locations."

He gives me a look when he says this, and I can't help feeling an underlying threat. What if no other facilities like Renascence exist? Is he implying that our discovery has less merit because another one can't be located or confirmed? It seems ridiculous to think that just because there may be only one place in the country creating a new human race, this is somehow less of a threat to our future.

However, it gives me pause as I consider this. Are people discounting the enormity of what we found because it's isolated? Is this why most of our efforts to publicize Ander's existence fail?

"Commander, what if Renascence is unique?" I ask, looking carefully at his features to assess his reaction. "There is a possibility that the work done there is the foundation of things to come. What if we can't locate another facility like that one?"

"We have considered that possibility, Enora. When we reassign you, you will not only be analyzing geographical data to locate other facilities. You will also be assisting our people in identifying what to look for in any incoming or outgoing communications, both historical and current. It seems highly unlikely that what you found hasn't at least been shared in various channels. General Malvolia's intelligence division is the first target, as she would have broad access to the inner workings of all operations across the state and possibly beyond."

As he talks, it is clear that his plans for Springer and I have been decided for some time. I wonder how long he's been mulling this over. Since before the raid? Or even earlier than that? I'm just a pawn, once again.

"When we finalize your placements, you will both be assigned a counterpart who will be responsible for you and will assist you in training operations at your future site. This should help you to assimilate more quickly into the ranks of your new division."

I want to shake my head in opposition. A counterpart? That's laughable. Better he just call it what it is, an informant, someone who will watch and report to make sure we follow orders and remain loyal.

"And Ander?" Springer's question makes my heart skip. Oh God, I had forgotten about the boy.

The commander's voice becomes harder, indicating that his statement is non-negotiable. "The boy will be sent to another branch as well. It's too risky to keep him here in close proximity to the raid, particularly in light of the general's recent communication. If he were apprehended, it would be catastrophic. His existence must become the face of our fight. When people truly understand the significance of what the DMC is creating, they will rise up and help us win this war."

CHAPTER TWENTY

I swallow my anger as Springer, and I make our way back to our quarters. The silence, and my slow progress, give me time to try to make sense of what we've been told and what the future holds. Panic is floating just below the surface of my thoughts, ready to emerge and cloud any reasoning. It's hard to push it away and look at the commander's edict with some rationality. Springer is equally quiet, no doubt muddled in his own thinking, though he is aware enough of me to slow his stride to match my uneven gait.

I sigh with relief when we finally reach our room. The door is ajar, and I can see that Hal and Ander are not here. This is a good thing, as we need time to talk and sort out how we're going to move forward. Ha. Like there's much we even need to discuss. It's not as though we have any say in where we go and what role we play. Those choices are not ours to make anymore. I chafe at that and relish the fury I feel building inside me.

Springer closes the door behind me as I hobble to my bed and sink into the softness. I moan in appreciation of the comfort, the position easing the throbbing of my leg. I watch as Springer sits across from me, his eyes traveling to my hand as it unconsciously rubs the aching muscles in my thigh.

As the pain begins to ebb, I break the silence. "You had a feeling something like this would happen, didn't you?"

"Not exactly. I knew that there was more than what we were told, some decision that had been discussed prior to yesterday's briefing. But this hadn't crossed my mind. Honestly, I had been thinking they were going to shuttle all three of us to a different location to drum up more support."

"I can't do this without you, Springer. I just..." I don't finish the thought. It's too hard to put words to how I feel. All I know is that without him, I am truly lost.

"You won't have to do this without me. I'm not letting you go. To hell with the resistance. You've seen what they do to people!"

"What do you mean?"

"I mean, they're the ones who blew up that town, Enora. Our side killed innocent people."

"What?" My mouth must be gaping open when I think about what he's saying.

"Do you remember that day when you asked Sergeant

Quinn why the DMC wasn't just bombing the towns with rebellions?"

"Yeah."

"I asked her about that when you were off training Farrel and Corin. You know what she said?"

I shake my head, not sure that I really want to hear.

"She told me that sometimes sacrifices had to be made to further the cause."

"But...did she mean the rebels did that?"

"She wouldn't say any more about it, but what else do you think she meant? The rebellion had all but died out, and they needed something to light the fire!"

"What kind of world do we live in, Springer? Has everyone gone mad?"

"I don't know. But we're going to get out of here."

"How?" I can't imagine leaving and getting very far in the wasteland we live in.

"We're going to do what Bram asked us to do. We'll follow his coordinates and find that lake."

Hope blooms in my heart when Springer says that. To find a place where water flows and truly be free is a concept that I can't even wrap my head around. But my hope is tinged with the cold reality of what it means to go off on our own.

"I haven't figured out how yet, but we won't have much time. They'll likely be anticipating some action on our part, and I expect that we'll be watched closely from now on." Springer lets out a frustrated breath. "This won't be easy, and with your leg, we'll be at a huge disadvantage. You're not very mobile, which means without a vehicle of some sort, we won't get far."

"Even without my injury, we wouldn't get far, Springer. Have you forgotten the wasteland we live in? Without the resistance or the Company, how do we survive? There's nothing out there. And if they're both hunting us..." The picture in my head is a bleak one. I see scenes drift through my memories, and it's always the same withered landscapes. Fifteen hundred miles is how far Bram told us we'd have to travel. It's a death sentence to go off on our own.

"We have to try, Enora. If they separate us, I'll never see you again. I made a promise to protect you."

"A promise to whom?"

"Bram."

The ache in my leg is suddenly eclipsed by the one in my heart. Bram exacted that promise from him. Even from the grave, he looks out for me, showing me the way. I pull up an image of him and hold it there in my mind. I can remember our conversation as I linger on his phantom face. We were sitting atop our favorite hill, enjoying our stolen moments. He was so young then, not like the hard man I encountered when all of this began. There were no lines of harsh living creasing his face, no reflections of too many evil deeds seen and done. We were young, and life was simpler. Together we built dreams of freedom and flowing rivers. How could we have known then what lay in store for us?

I've lived a lifetime since that day. Bram didn't end up protecting me from the ugliness. He made me face it.

Bram's face slowly fades as the present shifts back into focus. To try to leave is crazy. But I realize that I would rather risk it all than face a future without Springer, a future where I could end up as a puppet with a different master pulling the strings. I don't know what I'm fighting for anymore. Am I still trying to show the world the truth about a mutated race, or am I just struggling for my survival?

If I were truly here for the cause, wouldn't it make sense to go along with their plans and help shape the fighters in this burgeoning war? Isn't my bond with Springer worth losing if it means that the Company can be brought down? It's too much to think about. Part of me knows what's right and understands the gain is worth the cost, but the louder, angrier part refuses to compromise. I'm so tired of fighting.

"Springer, I don't know what's right and wrong anymore. I've lost sight of what I'm fighting for."

"We're fighting for the truth, Enora. The people need to see the truth. We've given Commander Guire facts about what the DMC is creating, but now we need to give the people hope. They deserve to know that the world isn't a wasteland. That's probably the biggest lie the Company has told."

"Will it matter?"

He looks taken aback by my question. "Of course, it will! Are you saying...what are saying?"

I rub my hand against my forehead, trying to gather my thoughts. "It just seems to me that we're taking all the risks, and no matter what they see, it isn't going to change anything. Why do *we* have to sacrifice so much? When will it be enough to get them, all of them, ready to stand up and fight for this world? Is it *ever* going to be enough?"

"Yes." He sounds so sure of himself. "What would you have done if you found out that all of the harsh restrictions you've lived with were a cover-up?"

"I would be mad as hell."

"Exactly. We need to do this."

I look away. "You're right. They should know there's hope. We can't stay here and let them tear us apart. I don't think I could do this, any of it." Gulping loudly, I force myself to say what I really feel. "I can't lose you. You're worth more to me than any of this." And that last part, that selfish admission, is my reality. Up to now, I've been able to go on without Bram and my parents, without Safa. But to lose Springer? There wouldn't be anything left if I let that happen.

"I know." He strokes my face, eyes filled with under-standing. "From my perspective, we've done our part, and now it's up to them to use what we've shared."

"We have to take Ander with us."

"Enora..."

I cut him off. "I won't leave him." He wants to argue with me. I can see it in his face. "It's our fault he's here. We can't leave him behind in the hands of someone like Kane."

"You know they aren't going to keep him here, Enora. He's not going to end up with Doctor Kane."

"Springer, I'm not leaving him with them to become some weaponized object they'll toss aside when he's no longer useful. If I do, then I've killed the last piece of me that has any humanity left. I will truly become a monster."

Springer stands up and paces in a small circle in our cramped quarters. "Taking him with us is going to be next to impossible. The rebels need him for the cause. He's the evidence that the Company wants to hide."

"He's not the only thing they're hiding. There's water out there. We must be able to find some way to make this work. We're not going to leave him behind."

"I don't know, Enora. He's an asset. They're not going to torture him or something when they need him. He's not expendable, like us. He'll be safer and better off here."

"He trusts us, Springer. Without us, he's just a means to an end. When he's given them all he can, what's going to happen?"

Springer can't hide his frustration. "Look, what you're talking about is suicide. There's no way in hell that Commander Guire will let this go. He'll hunt us down, just like the Company is hunting us."

"He won't be able to find us."

He runs his hands through his hair and then slowly drags them across his face. I know he's done arguing with me. "You've got whatever time we have left before they begin to put things in place, to try to come up with a plan that you can convince me of. If we run out of time, we're leaving. Just the two of us. I'm not going to make this a suicide mission just to save that kid."

"Okay." I know what I need to do to get ready, and it's going to require something I detest: sucking up and playing the role of a good little soldier. But if I do it right, we'll have a chance.

Springer leaves, and I begin to compile a mental list of what I'll need to learn about the rebel communications and security systems to be able to hack them and escape. If I can buy us enough time to get out undetected, then we'll have a chance to make it far enough for the resistance to abandon the idea of pursuit.

First, I'll need to put on my mask of compliance and educate myself. Faking it is not a task I'm at all good at, and I worry that Dade, the head of technology here, will see right through me. Hal and Ander walk in as I'm working myself into a panic attack.

I guess my face must've looked rather green because Hal immediately asks, "Are you alright? Is it your leg?"

"Yeah, it's pretty sore today," I say and jerk my head to the corner of the room.

Hal catches my meaning. Ander scampers over to me,

gives me an affectionate pat on the back, and then plops down with his gadgets.

Hal and I step into the corner of the room. It's cramped, but I don't want what I have to say to go beyond these walls. As I'm about to launch into a complicated explanation of what is going on, I feel Springer's censure from a distance. He wouldn't want me telling Hal anything, but Springer doesn't understand the bond that is created between an adult and a child. I know I can trust Hal. He wouldn't want Ander falling into anyone's hands who may do him harm.

In hushed tones, I lay it all out for him, everything, from our roles within the DMC to Bram, my parents, and Safa, ending with Commander Guire's decision. When I get to that part of the story, Hal looks stricken. I follow it up with the hidden lake, that beacon of hope. Hal's face lights up, and I know I've made the right choice.

"We need your help, Hal. I can't let him fall into someone else's hands. You know what they'll do to him."

"You need to escape and find that lake," Hal whispers.

I nod. "Can you help us?"

"As a matter of fact, I can."

CHAPTER TWENTY-ONE

Springer nearly loses it when I tell him about my conversation with Hal. His expression is thunderous, and I feel like he wants to throttle me, but I continue talking, and gradually his face becomes less mottled, and his breathing returns to normal.

"Enora," he sighs and shakes his head. "You know, I always thought I'd die in some assignment gone wrong, but that's not going to happen. *You're* going to do that all on your own by giving me a heart attack one of these days."

"Ha ha," I mutter.

Springer begins walking in slow, small circles, digesting what I've told him. While I've been here with Hal, Springer began a serious reconnaissance of the compound. He's been busy locating various exit points in addition to supply rooms. Of course, he exudes an air of confidence, so no one thinks twice about his presence in various locations. If I were doing that, I'm sure someone would confront me.

"This could work," he finally concedes.

We spend the next couple of hours making our plans. It's decided that we'll need to leave sooner rather than later. We can't help feeling like the clock's ticking, and the longer we are here, the riskier it gets. Being an engineer of sorts, Hal has access to the various resistance vehicles, one of which is a solar-powered jeep. It hasn't worked in years, but Hal is convinced he can get it up and running as he's been tinkering with it for months. Without that kind of transportation, we would only get part of the way before running out of battery power.

I still need to do my part and learn how to interrupt the rebel's security system so we can get out of here unde-tected. Springer walks me to the communications room, and I see Dade sitting in front of a screen, shoulders and neck hunched like a tortoise. I think he may be farsighted because his face is so close to the screen that I can't imagine any normally sighted person being able to read anything from that distance. I hobble over to a chair near Dade and clear my throat. He looks up, surprise stamped across his face. Clearly. he was so engrossed in his work that he didn't even hear me enter.

"Oh, hello." His voice is squeaky, which fits his small frame and buggish eyes.

"Hi. Commander Guire may have told you that I will be working with different teams and need some training." I sound like an idiot. My voice is too high, and I'm talking too fast. It's stupid to feel nervous. What I've said is true. It's just that I know that I'm going to be using this knowledge to betray the resistance, and I feel like the lie must be there, in my voice or face.

"Yes, he did tell me. Before we get started, why don't you tell me what you already know about software systems, and we'll go from there."

It's a long afternoon, and my eyes are blurry from looking at the screen for so long by the time I'm done. As I stand up shakily, Dade reaches out a hand to steady me. "You're a quick learner, Enora."

I feel a weight of guilt when he compliments me but manage to respond with what I hope is a normal tone. "Thanks, Dade. You're a good teacher." It'll be hard to betray one of the good guys.

He smiles and helps me to the doorway. From there, I wave goodbye and use the walls for support as I make my way back to my room. I really meant what I said to him. He's a great teacher. In the hours we spent pouring over code, I learned much more than I had anticipated. Thankfully, my previous training and assignments allowed me to absorb this new information quickly, and I feel confident that I can apply it when I need to. The rebel security systems aren't so different from the ones I've been trained to hack.

When Hal surprises me with a small computer system

he put together from scraps, I give him a sincere smile. "Thank you, Hal!"

"You're welcome. I thought it would be better if you had your own equipment and didn't take something the people here might need to keep them safe."

"You're a good man, Hal. I'm glad you thought of this. I do need it and feel much better not having to take something that could get people killed."

He smiles and sits down next to Ander, who's been tinkering with yet another gadget Hal made for him. I smile fondly at the two and then focus on Hal's unexpected gift.

As the computer screen illuminates, I can see that he's got some basic software on there, most likely on a drive he salvaged when he put it together. I pull the machine onto my lap and begin uploading systems I'll need, plus others that may come in handy. I'm even more grateful to Dade for showing me so much as I work. The time I spent with him is invaluable as he inadvertently showed me multiple backdoors into the rebel's system. I push aside a brief feeling of guilt and refocus my energy on the task at hand.

Hal has been talking quietly to Springer as I work, and my attention is suddenly grabbed by what he says. "You're going to need me to go with you."

It's clear from Springer's face that this is not an option he'd like to consider.

Hal holds up his hand before Springer begins to voice his objections. "Look, you need a driver. Unless you can coordinate stocking the vehicle with supplies, getting the three of you to the garage and into it, while simultaneously hacking into the security system to open up the garage itself and keeping watch for anyone who may see you, then this is going to fail."

"How exactly would you be able to help us?" Springer asks.

"I've already got the vehicle and can begin stocking it at any time so that when we need to leave, it'll be ready. When it's time, I can drive while you and Enora cover our tracks." I can't help but notice the term 'we'. He starts to fidget, clearly nervous at having this conversation. Admittedly, I'm rather impressed by his courage. If he's going to join us, he'll need all the nerve he can gather. "If you leave me here, I'm a dead man."

Hal is right, we need him, and I don't want any else's blood on my hands. "Springer." He looks over at me. "He's right."

On reflection, I confess that our trio becoming a quartet is going to make all of this much easier. With Hal, we have a much better chance of escaping in the first place, plus he's a fix-it kind of guy, and that could end up as a big help.

THE DAY WE DECIDE TO LEAVE IS TEN DAYS AFTER Safa died. It's hard to believe that so much has changed since that moment. For the first time, I will have a true taste of freedom, but it's a bittersweet victory.

Our timing is well coordinated. Commander Guire and Sergeant Quinn have left to meet with the other divisions that we will be sent to, and though it's silly, I can't help feeling like we have a better chance with them away.

Springer's been smuggling supplies over the last few days, and Hal has hidden them in the vehicle we'll be taking. Of course, they won't last us too long, but it won't matter once we reach the water. We decide to leave midday, a time when most of the division will be taking a break for lunch or rest. Springer, Ander and I, head to a seldom-used corridor in an upper level. It's a bit of a hike, but from there, we can make our way above ground.

The passages are dimly lit. Springer has Ander perched in the same carrier he used when we stole him from Renascence. I warned Ander about being absolutely quiet before we left, and I can see him working to be silent as we make our way. I watch him closely and put my finger to my lips when I see him turn toward me. I'm rewarded with a small grin. It's good he doesn't understand the severity of what we're doing. If it goes wrong, I hope it'll be quick.

"I always knew you'd turn traitor." A snide voice echoes into the dimness.

Springer and I spin around and come face to face with Piper. Rage surges through me as I stare at her, but I am in control this time. Feigning a look of fright, I push Springer away from me, hoping he'll get the hint and move backward to give me space. My expression must be convincing because Piper saunters toward me, confident and careless.

I wait and watch her approach. "Please, Piper," I say breathlessly, infusing a pleading into my voice.

"*Please?*" She shakes her head. "You're going down. No one makes a fool of me and gets away with it. I already took care of that traitor friend of yours. Now it's your turn."

I hold my anger in check and let her continue to move toward me. Then, when she's only a couple of feet away, I lunge, taking her off guard and bringing her to the ground. I hear Springer talking to Ander and quickly moving away. When I no longer hear his footsteps, I let loose my wrath.

By the time it's finished, all that's left is her limp form sprawled in an unconscious heap. I stand up slowly, wiping the blood off my knuckles. I didn't kill her, though I was close. No. She'll have to live with the knowledge that I got away. Despite her, I escaped and avenged Safa.

CHAPTER TWENTY-TWO

We make it above ground without further incident. As soon as the three of us crouch in the blinding sun, I let out a pent-up breath in a long whoosh. My knuckles ache. I smile in grim satisfaction at the pain. Flexing my fingers, I churn up some spit and wipe away the blood crusted in the creases of my skin. I want nothing of Piper tainting me. I am done with her and put her actions in the past, where they belong.

Springer is quietly watching me as I clean up. I know he understands my actions, maybe even supports them. Regardless, it's done. The hand of justice was dealt.

"Break anything, slugger?"

I crack a smile. "I'm too tough for that, and she was too soft."

He chuckles. I give Ander, who's looking at my hands

with wide eyes, a quick look to try to assess what he may have seen. "Enora had a nosebleed, Ander. You ever get one?"

Continuing to stare at me, Ander shakes his head. "I never got one, but Jago used to get them lots of times."

I vaguely recall Ander talking about Jago, one of the 'bad kids'. It's like small pieces of a puzzle keep falling into place as I learn more about who Ander is and what he saw while in Renascence. Like the violent behavior he mentioned when telling me about Jago, perhaps nosebleeds were a physical side effect of his mutation. If so, I wonder in how many other ways these mutations are evident. Did anyone do any long-term study? I mentally shake my head, not likely. And this brings me back to one of my many worries.

Is Renascence the first of its kind? If so, will the work people brush it off?

My thoughts are interrupted by the sound of a vehicle approaching. We crouch lower, and I tell Ander, "Don't make a sound, okay?"

He nods and clamps a hand over his mouth. I give him a thumbs-up and then look toward the whine of an electric engine. Springer reaches over and grabs my hand, giving it a squeeze. The action says so much. My throat feels tight as I squeeze back.

Speeding in our general direction is a type of jeep. As it gets closer, I feel Springer relax and know it's Hal. We stand up and wave Hal over. He swings around, spraying dirt that coats my clothes and stings my eyes. I wipe it away and yank open the door.

Once we're in, Springer says, "Great work, Hal! Anyone following you?"

"I don't think so. I disabled the vehicles so no one would be able to track us down, at least not right away. I didn't want to disable anything permanently."

I pat him on the shoulder as we speed away, heading north. "How'd you do that?"

Hal grins. "Pulled a few wires here and there."

Springer and I laugh, and I relax into the seat, relishing my first real taste of freedom. No tracers. No Company spies. No resistance. Just us.

Ander burrows next to me. "Did our adventure start, Enora?"

I see Hal look at me in the rearview mirror, and I give him a smile. "It sure did."

Prior to our escape, I poured over maps to find the best routes toward the border with the smallest chance of contact. We manage to avoid encounters with DMC personnel as we travel into the afternoon. This means taking numerous unmarked roads, dusty, winding routes that make me feel a bit queasy as the hours pass. Our goal is to get to an unpopulated valley between Brigford and Filmont, about five hundred miles away.

From what I was able to see from older satellite

images, there are no towns left in this location, having been absorbed into the two nearby cities and those larger settlements on the outskirts. My worry is what the maps couldn't show me: any hubs of the resistance that may be lurking beneath the surface in old mining shafts, pipelines, or abandoned military installations. It's a risk, but this whole endeavor is.

A couple of hours into the drive, we've stopped and are stretching our legs when Springer spots a patrol. "Get the car farther off the road, Hal. Slowly so we don't make any dust. Enora, get Ander and hide under that outcrop of rocks."

Having been prepared for this inevitability, we had stopped in an area with good shelter. Hal squeezes the jeep into a shadowy crevice between a couple of giant boulders. Unable to open the doors to get out, he remains in the vehicle while the three of us hide.

"Did they see us?" I whisper.

"No. They were really far off, but I could see the dust cloud from their passing."

I tell Ander to be still and quiet and strain my ears for the sound of the patrol. Twenty minutes pass, and we hear nothing other than a distant rumble.

Springer cocks his head and turns to me. "Stay here."

He hikes to a small rise, going onto his stomach at the top, and scans the horizon in all directions. I let out a breath of relief when he straightens and jogs back.

"They're gone, but I want to stay here a little longer just to be sure another patrol doesn't come by."

"Okay," I tell him. "I'll let Hal know."

I knock on the jeep's rear window, and Hal opens the hatch. "They're gone, but Springer wants to wait it out a bit to make sure it's safe."

"That's a relief. I'm going to climb out the back and join you."

The remainder of our break is a quiet, calm time, our nerves having been rattled. It's becoming so real now. If we're caught, no one will save us.

The sun is setting when we finally arrive in the valley. Rather than scoping it out from a high vantage point and making ourselves a target, we head straight down along a wide depression that may have been carved out by water long ago. I can't help the parched ache that fills my mouth at the thought of free-flowing water cutting through rock and dirt. It must have been beautiful. Once we make it to the west side of the valley floor, Hal stops the jeep, so I can hop out and find a high spot to view the area. Having permanently borrowed it from Sergeant Quinn's division, I take out my scope and locate the best spot to make camp. It's a section of the valley dotted with large boulders and scraggly shrubs, perfect for hiding our encampment.

It doesn't take long to set up. Springer makes a series of lean-tos with brown canvas covers he pilfered from some storage room. These will provide protection from prying eyes and the sun, plus they blend well with the color of the earth and rocks. Ander is filled with excitement, hopping from rock to rock and digging in the dirt.

Even this late in the day, the heat is oppressive, and my mouth feels as dry as the cracked earth. An ache in my stomach compounds my thirst. It's been hours since we had anything to eat. I hobble to a soft area and stretch out my aching leg under the tarp, letting my body lean against the warmth of a large boulder.

My belly rumbles. If I had any spit left, my mouth would be watering at the thought of eating one of the stale protein bars Springer stole. Instead, I watch as Springer digs into one of our bags, taking out just enough for each of us to have half a bar. It's depressing to know that I'll still feel ravenous after eating. Hal hands me his cup of water. For a moment, I'm filled with surprise and pleasure as it's a large container, but when I look inside, I see it's only a quarter full.

Hal notices my disappointment. "Sorry. I wish it could be more."

"It's okay. We need to conserve what we have until we get there." I take a small sip and hand it back.

Mentally, I picture the blue water of the lake, Bram's lake as I've started to call it. I imagine the sensation of falling into it and gulping mouthfuls. For a few minutes, I close my eyes and just let myself live in the moment. We've done it. Against the odds, we've made it this far. It fills me with hope.

I must have fallen asleep because the next thing I

know is Ander is shaking me awake. "You snored." His nose wrinkles at this, as though the noise must've been loud and annoying.

"Oh, yeah? Maybe that was just your stomach rumbling."

"Nah-ah. That was you!" He says as he pokes me in the arm.

It's easier to laugh with him here and smile a genuine smile. "Okay, okay. You got me. I was snoring. Did I drool?" I wipe my chin, pretending to clear away the evidence.

Ander bursts into little giggles. "Yuck!"

"Help me up, kid." I reach out my arms, and Ander' helps' by pulling me up, though, in reality, he's much too small. The muscles in my leg scream in protest at the movement, and I suck in a breath before shuffling forward like an old woman.

Springer and Hal are squatting comfortably in the center of our little camp, each with a small cup of water. I know without looking that they are less than a quarter full. My throat feels like it's caked in dirt as I make my way over.

Pointing with a wave of my finger, I ask, "Got one for me?"

Springer reaches into his pack, pulling out my all-too-familiar cup, a battered thing we took on every assignment. There are so many memories tied to this hunk of metal. I cradle it in my hands and lean over so Springer can give me my ration. It takes all my willpower to sip slowly, savoring every drop so that it lasts.

I look over and find Ander plopped on the ground playing with a stick. "Ander, are you thirsty?"

He looks over at me. "Uh-huh."

Springer scoots over so I can sit next to him, but I shake my head, needing to stand and stretch my quivering muscles. "Any sign of a patrol?"

Springer takes a small sip from his cup, then answers. "Not yet. The eastern border of the valley is about half a mile away, and from what I can see, there's nothing out here. You picked a good spot, Enora. There's good cover, and it's far enough from everything that I don't think we'll see a DMC presence."

It's relieving to hear that. "Do you think we'll make it in two days?"

"That's a good question," Springer pauses and thinks it over. "I guess it depends on whether or not we run into any trouble."

What none of us say is that if we're spotted, they'll run us down. There would be no escape, no matter whose hands we fall into.

CHAPTER TWENTY-THREE

The dawn is beautiful when it comes. I sit perched on a large boulder up the hill from our camp. As the colors flood the sky, I realize that it's been years since I've watched the sunrise. Light fills the horizon with hues of orange and pink, then golden yellow. I let my mind go where it will. I think of Bram and Safa and all that they stood for. I remember my parents and how they worked so hard under the yoke of an entity that cared nothing for them, killing them in the end.

Safa, in her way, had always fought against the Company. She saw their control as a burden and took such a risk to create something that would've made life better for everyone if only the DMC would've allowed it. After I've seen and done so much, it's only now that I can truly appreciate why she never accepted what this life had given her.

And Bram. It still hurts to think of him. I will never know how it truly began for Bram. When did he first realize that the Company, and all it stood for, was a lie? How long did he plan for me to join him? I wish he could've told me. I wish he hadn't turned me into a killer. But then, I wouldn't be here now if I hadn't seen and done all that I have. I miss him. I miss them all.

I can see Springer packing our gear in my peripheral, his movements efficient, born of years of practice. As he works, I take time to truly appreciate everything that he's done, through his assignments as Sweeper to working for both sides to taking on the role of my protector and friend. He's a good man, despite what he thinks. I know there is blood on his hands. Unseen though they may be, the stains are there. I have them too, and no amount of washing will ever rid me of them. It's the price we've paid to see that the powerful are truly corrupt on all sides.

I watch Springer come to me and sit down by my side. Part of him remains a mystery that I've never really thought to solve. He's so independent, so self-assured. That must have come from experience. "Springer, what happened to your family?"

"They died. I have no family." Springer says this so matter-of-factly that I don't know how to respond.

"I know they died, but did the DMC do that?" He makes a face, so I add, "You don't need to talk about it if it bothers you. I don't mean to be nosy."

"It's okay. They've been gone a long time. In a way, yes,

the Company is responsible. But not how you'd think. I guess I could blame them for the heartlessness of their actions, but I also understand why they did what they did."

My brows crease as I try to interpret what he means as he continues. "My town was one of those hit by the first X3 outbreak. It spread so quickly that the Company quarantined the whole town. By the time the virus had run its course, nearly half the people were dead, my parents among them. Those of us left behind were relocated. I was young to be recruited, but that's where they placed me."

"Why didn't you ever tell me that before?"

He shrugs. "You never asked. Honestly, it's not something I like to remember or talk about. But, when I think about it, I can still smell that stink of sickness and misery. That kind of death has a scent that never really leaves you."

I feel guilty at never really asking about the details of his life before all of this. It's strange, really. When I think about it, I've been rather closed mouth myself. It's almost as though there was nothing before all of this. I wonder if that is intentional. I think it must be.

When training began, the DMC became the guiding force in my life. All communication was cut off until I'd earned the privilege to call home, and returning for visits was not a likely option no matter how I impressed them. When I look at it that way, I can't feel too bad that I never talked or wondered about his life before the DMC. That period may as well have been someone else's life. Now, it's just us.

Springer straightens and scans the area until he finds me. "Time to head out."

"I'm ready." I reach out my arms, and he gently hauls me to my feet, holding onto me a little longer than he needs to.

Cupping my face, his eyes glow as he looks down at me. "I'll go anywhere with you, Enora. Be anything for you."

"I know," I whisper.

And then something seems to click into place. I open my mouth and let words I've never said come out. "I loved him, Springer, with all my heart, but I never let him know, not really. I'm not going to make that mistake again. I love you."

I reach up, hands trembling in uncertainty, and pull his face down to mine. Clumsily, I press my lips to his. They are cracked from too much sun and too little moisture, but to me, his mouth is soft and warm. His lips claim mine in a deeper kiss, one I'm unprepared for but helpless to resist, and while it only lasts a few moments, it changes me. Allowing the barriers I've spent years building to come crashing down, I accept that Springer is everything to me now. I can only hope that I deserve him.

"I love you too, Enora. More than you know."

Springer pulls me down the hill toward our camp,

holding my hand. Nothing has changed. Our course is set, and our goals remain. Yet, everything is different.

My legs quickly feel like jelly at the strain of the hurried downward trek. I hadn't realized how far I'd gone, and I'm using muscles I didn't seem to feel too much on my way up this hill. Pain burrows so deeply into my bones that it feels like a living thing. I want to sink to my knees in fatigue but settle for pulling on his hand to slow my descent.

"Wait. I don't think I can take another step."

"I could sling you over my shoulder and haul you down." He comments with a wink.

"I bet you would, slave driver." I shift into a sitting position and stretch my leg out, embracing the discomfort. It's a good kind of pain.

"I want you to rest here a moment while I do a quick perimeter check to make sure it's safe to head out."

I salute him and lay back, sighing in pleasure as my muscles begin to relax. I fix my gaze on the blueness of the sky, hearing the soft patter of Springer's feet as he quietly makes a circuit. As I lie there listening to him, I want to touch my lips, just to have some proof that our kiss was real, but I settle for licking them with a tongue that sticks to my skin.

Mistaking my actions, Springer stands over me and asks, "Hungry?"

I am, actually. "I'm starving."

"Come on, let's get some breakfast." He helps me up,

and we make our way down to camp, only having to stop
one other time so I can rest my leg.

Ander is chattering away to Hal when I limp into the
center of camp but stops when he sees me. "Where'd you
go, Enora? Into the bushes to pee?"

"Nah. I was just watching the sunrise with Springer."

"There's lots of colors when the sun wakes up."

"There sure are. Did you eat something, Ander?"

"Hal gave me half his breakfast, but I'm still hungry.
Are you gonna give me half of yours?"

Springer looks at Ander. "Enora's got to share with me,
kid."

"Oh. But I'm still hungry."

"How about I give you a bite of mine, okay?"

I can see Springer giving me 'a look' so I stick my
tongue out at him and grab our breakfast, breaking off a
small piece of my half before he can stop me. Ander pops
it into his mouth and chews in satisfaction.

When Ander's attention drifts back to Hal, I gingerly
sit next to Springer and begin eating slowly. It's important
to take my time and chew for as long as I can. It fools my
stomach into thinking I'm getting more.

I'm not much help when it comes time to pack. My leg
is aching so badly that I worry I've done some damage.
Finding a sheltered spot, I pull down my pants and look
under the bandage. I can see blood, and I bite my lip as I
roll the gauze down to get a better look. Four of the

stitches are torn out, the result of trekking up and down the hill this morning.

Springer finds me like that, pants down and bloody. "Um, Enora?"

My head flops forward in embarrassment. "Could you please turn around? I'm not dressed."

"Yeah, I can see that." But he doesn't leave. Instead, he gets closer, peering down at my leg.

I press my hand to the front of my underwear. "Springer! Go away!"

"Hey, I'm not looking there."

I slant my eyes at him. "Really? You could've fooled me."

"Well, I mean, I looked, but I'm not..." His face begins to turn a dull red. "Look, do you want some help or what?"

"Fine, you perv. Can you get me some antiseptic? My stitches tore."

"You got it. Just keep those pants down, and I'll be right back." He laughs at my gasp of outrage and trots away.

By the time he's finished cleaning me up, I'm placed on severely restricted duty. So while Springer and Hal finish packing up camp, I sit and watch Ander play with rocks.

Springer jogs over to me with his lanky stride when everything is loaded. Just beyond the jeep, Hal calls Ander over, and the two of them toss a rag ball Hal made for the boy.

Springer pulls me gently to my feet so I don't accidentally pull out any more stitches. "Ready?"

"Yep." But he makes no move to get into the jeep. His fingers stroke my hands and trail up my arms. There's something about this moment that transcends the nerves pulsing through me, something deeper, with a tinge of sadness.

"Are you okay?" I almost don't want to hear his reply, nervous that he senses something. He says nothing, only touches me.

"Springer?" I ask, unable to stop the worry in my voice.

"I'm just thinking."

"About what?"

"You."

I tilt my head, so I can look in his face. He reaches over and strokes my lower lip with his thumb. I feel it catch on the chapped roughness.

"Enora, no matter what happens, I need you to know I wouldn't change a thing. All I've done, everything we've been a part of, has led me here, to you. For so long, it's just been me. I haven't needed anyone, haven't wanted anyone either, if I'm being honest." I open my mouth, and he puts his fingers against it, keeping me from uttering a word. "I don't know what's waiting for us when we reach the end of this journey. But, whatever it is, it was worth it."

He's rarely so serious, and it worries me. "Springer, what are you saying?"

"You need to promise me something."

I feel wary of making a promise before I know what he's asking of me. "Can you tell me what I'm promising?"

"Don't risk your life for me. If it comes to it, you need to run. You need to leave me behind and save yourself."

"What?" I pull back, unable to stop myself. "You can't ask me to leave you. I can't do that. Not after everything that's happened. No. I won't."

"Enora, listen to me. What's the point of all of this if you give up?"

"Springer, don't..."

"No, you listen. What did Bram die for, huh? If things go badly, you can't let them take you. You have to run."

"That's not going to happen. We're going to finish this together. You and me, we're going to find that lake, and we'll swim and drink water until we're sick. We'll be free. I don't want that without you. I can't have it without you." Inside, all I can think of is what each day would look like if Springer weren't by my side. It's such a desolate thought.

"Enora, this is bigger than us."

"No."

"Yes. Bram wanted us to find this place and tell the world, to give them hope for the future and show them the lies that have been told for so long. That was his wish."

"I can't leave you, Springer. Don't make me promise that."

He cups my face. "Do you remember how you felt when you realized that the Company is creating a mutation?"

"Yes. I was horrified."

"What do you think their reasons are behind it?" His eyes plead with mine.

"Ander's kind is better suited for this world."

Springer nods. "His kind is designed for the world the DMC controls, a place of strict rations and ultimate control. But they are hiding more than his creation. Just imagine the place Bram told us about. If it rains there and the water never dries up, then the Aurora Strain isn't a way to save humanity. There's no need to create something like Ander if there's enough water to sustain the rest of us."

I find his logic confusing. "What are you saying?"

"The world deserves to know everything. They need to understand that the DMC is keeping them under control, not because the world is a desert, but hoarding what they have."

What he says makes sense, but there's still a missing part. "Then why create Ander at all?"

He gives me a sad smile. "Because when the rest of us are gone, his kind will thrive. A species specially designed to live and flourish within their rigid control. They'll be able to inhabit every pocket of this world. To them, the scarcity we struggle with will be nonexistent. Imagine how much easier it will be for the DMC if the populace is complacent and feel no strain at the rationing and hardships. They won't fight it as we have. They also won't use so much of a resource that is scarce enough that we have no lakes and rivers in much of the country."

"But, in Renascence, his kind had plenty." I point out.

"That's just the breeding ground. When his kind have been perfected..."

He doesn't finish the thought, but I can imagine the new world he's envisioning. It's a place completely devoid of humans.

I watch his mouth curve in a small smile, one that's tinged in sadness, when I agree. "You're right. What we're trying to do is bigger than us. I promise to run if it comes to that. I'll take Ander and run, but you have to make the same promise."

His eyes flash in a spasm of pain. "I do."

It is a pledge neither of us wants to face, but I've found that this life often doesn't give us a chance to avoid the tough choices.

These strange days
Bring hard choices
Realities
We thought we knew
Promises
We tried to keep
It all changes
In the moment
That clarity comes
That second
When the truth
Finally reveals itself

CHAPTER TWENTY-FOUR

It feels as though we've been driving for weeks by the time we reach the next location to camp. We've traveled almost a thousand miles, taking numerous back routes to avoid any contact with patrols. Aside from a drone we spotted while stopped for a quick lunch, there have been no incidents. It's almost more frightening not having seen anything. It makes it feel as though trouble is just waiting around the corner, biding its time. Hal parks the jeep under a huge jut of rock. It's a good spot as we can drape the canvas covers over the edge, and there'll be room for everything, including the four of us.

When all necessary gear is unloaded, I hunt down some food, my stomach snarling. Digging into a bag, I pull out a container with the last of our mix of synthetic beef jerky, nuts, and some dried fruit. There is just enough for each of us to have a large handful. I pass it around, careful not to spill. For Ander, I put his smaller share in a cup so he can eat it without dropping any in the dirt. We are silent for a good five minutes, the only sound that of soft chewing with an occasional crunch.

As I eat, I begin to worry about the supplies we have left. Springer didn't take much when he raided the stores at the rebel base. I don't blame him for grabbing so little. Those people were nearly starving, and I wouldn't want to be responsible for anyone suffering because we literally took food from their mouths. But having so little to start with and not much left has got me worried. What if the area around the lake doesn't have any food sources? I don't know what's beyond the border, no maps having shown anything past that point.

I'm about to ask Springer his thoughts when Ander hops up, having already finished eating, and comes running toward me. "Enora, wanna see how fast I can run?"

I raise my eyebrows, having no idea how this child could get that much energy from such a small meal. "Sure, but don't go too far."

"I won't," he assures and goes bounding off, looking back at me often to make sure I'm watching.

It hurts a little to look at him and see his sweet innocence, to know that until recently, I've just been using him as a means to an end, to face the fact that I was no better than Commander Guire, not really. Ander's so sincere, his open face and guileless smile. In contrast, I have been playing two parts: one a dutiful caregiver and the other a traitor using every weapon I have at my disposal. What happened with the rebels shone a spotlight on whom I was using and what it meant. Before that, I hadn't questioned the morality of my choices.

I look back on my path. A route laid out before me with hidden intent. Bram trusted me to find a way, see the true face of our enemy, and use my knowledge for the greater good. Ander is part of that now. He's not some weapon for the resistance to use. I feel a piece of my humanity return as I look at the child run toward me. Bram would be proud. So would my parents, I think.

Barely winded, Ander comes to a skidding stop in front of me, kicking up dirt. "Did you see how fast I ran?"

I crouch down to be at eye level with him. "I sure did!" I ruffle his hair and watch as he skips over to Springer, trying to impress him with tales of prowess.

Springer chuckles and engages with Ander in his easy way. The evening wanes, and despite being stuck in a jeep all day, I feel exhausted.

Hal looks at me as my eyes start to droop. He must see the lines of fatigue and what I can only assume are dark circles casting shadows under my eyes. "You're beat. You both are. Let me take care of Ander, and you two get an early rest."

I get up and head to my thin sleeping pad, curling up on my good side as I listen to the low hum of Hal and Springer's voices. My mouth feels pasty, and I smack my lips, wishing I could have another ration of water. Sleep comes despite the discomfort, the stress of the journey having drained me both physically and mentally.

Sometime during the night, I hear the high-pitched whine of a drone flying overhead. I bolt upright and feel Springer do the same. My heart pounds, and it becomes hard for me to hear the noise of the drone. I feel Springer squeeze my hand. There's nothing we can do if they see us. Nowhere we could hide that they won't find us.

Finally, the sound becomes distant, and we collapse into each other's arms. Fear has robbed me of the will to speak, so I just hold tightly to him, wishing I could burrow into his strength. Somehow, we manage to fall back to sleep, locked together. Hours later, I awaken to feel Springer's arm cushioning my head. I turn toward him, slowly so that I don't strain my leg, and look at his face.

His mouth is lax in sleep, lines of worry gone, giving him a boyish look. Admiring him, I begin to appreciate how hard his life has been. It's in his eyes that you see it, hard when they need to be and soft when he can no longer hide it. In sleep, he is young and untroubled. After the terror of last night, I drink him in, not wanting to waste a moment of our time together.

Springer must feel the weight of my stare because he opens his eyes, giving me a lazy smile. "Hey."

I lean forward, kissing his rough mouth softly. "Hi."

He stretches, his neck and back giving off a series of pops as he works out the kinks. "Are you okay?"

"I am now."

He kisses my lips and rests his face on the top of my head, tucking me under his chin. "We were lucky."

"Yeah."

He strokes my back in rhythmic circles. "I suppose it's time to pack up and finish this journey."

I prop my head on my hand and look at him, reluctant to move. Our moments are so fleeting. I wonder if we'll be able to slow it down, really be with each other, when we finally make it to the lake. Springer gives me one last kiss on the forehead, then stands and reaches for me to help me up. His hands stroke my arms and hug my waist as I get my feet under me while my leg screams in protest. Hal sees that we're up and ambles away with Ander, giving us whatever time he can. With a few last touches and whispered words, we pack up our emotions and focus on reaching our destination.

Ander is crabby when Springer piles him into the jeep after a meager breakfast and cup of water we all had to share. He's tired of the constant travel, and I can't blame him. Hal sits next to him, pulling him close and distracting him with a series of tickles. It's such a fatherly action. I sit in the passenger seat, and Springer drives slowly out of our campground toward Ashland, a town at the base of the mountain range we need to cross to get beyond the border. According to my map, there is an old logging road still in use. We'll need to take that up the mountain to a narrow crevasse and then go on foot the rest of the way. It's too heavily patrolled to try to take the road up and over the mountain. From Bram's coordinates, the lake is in a valley on the other side of the range. If we cut through the narrow ravine, it's a relatively easy hike to get there, and we have a greater chance of not being seen.

By noon, we've made it to the Ashland area. Wary of getting too close to the small town, we skirt the perimeter by a few dozen miles, taking back roads and then no roads at all.

"When are we gonna stop, Hal?" I hear Ander whine for what must be the tenth time.

Ever patient, Hal reassures him. "Real soon. You see that mountain? We've got to drive up it a ways, and then we'll stop."

"But I'm hungry, and I'm tired of sitting!"

Hal looks at me as I crane my neck to see the two of them and asks, "Can I give him some food?"

I think about how little we have left. But Ander is squirming, and I don't want him to keep complaining. "He could eat the last of the crackers. They're in the bag behind your seat."

Hal reaches back and quickly rifles through it to find the crackers. Only four remain, and he looks at me with worry. I return the look, but we both know there's nothing we can do. Ander claps his hands when Hal gives him the food and quickly digs in.

It is with a huge amount of unease that we make our way onto the logging road. It is one way, and if a patrol comes through, we'll have nowhere to go. The jeep is quiet as we begin the slow ascent. The crevasse we need to reach is about halfway up, and we'll need to leave the vehicle. That is a problem in itself, as we don't want to just ditch it out in the open. But we'll tackle that problem when we get to it.

There is a small pull-off we swing into when Ander starts complaining about needing to use the bathroom. Knowing how infrequently he goes, I know it's an issue if he's asking and that he won't be able to hold it. We all pile out to stretch, me with more care, as I'm so stiff.

Springer takes charge of Ander. "Come on, kid. Let's go find us some bushes."

Ander grabs his hand, and they head into the sparse terrain. "You gotta go too?"

"I sure do. I've been holding it even longer than you."

Their voices drift off, and it becomes quiet. From up here, I can see huge swaths of land. For a moment, I'm reminded of the view Bram, and I enjoyed back in Prineville.

"I've almost made it," I whisper to myself, to Bram, wishing he were here with me. Wishing he could know that I didn't give up.

I'm so lost in my thoughts that the sound of an engine doesn't register right away. But when it finally pierces my thoughts, I leap up, heart lodged in my throat. Hal comes running over, panic in his eyes.

"Oh God," I cry.

Hal shakes his head and looks around frantically. Springer comes charging out of the bushes, Ander hanging from his side in a tight grip. He swings the boy to his feet and shoves him into Hal's arms.

"Take him!"

Hal hauls Ander into a clump of bushes a dozen yards away, and they crawl under. Springer and I race to the jeep. He releases the brake, and we push it a few feet farther from the road into a copse of large bushes, hoping that the oncoming patrol will drive right by as they head down the mountain. Ander and Hal are flat on the ground looking at us. Springer signals that they stay put and slowly makes his way to a better vantage point.

I follow him, unable to remain behind. The sound is growing louder, and I know that they'll be on top of us within a few minutes. If they get close enough and scan the area, there's little chance of avoiding notice.

Reaching out, I yank on Springer's shirt, tugging hard to get him to stop. He looks back, and I see the panic in his eyes that I feel in my heart. We're trapped. If we run, they'll overtake us, calling in reinforcements from the air. If we stay, we're easy targets if we're spotted. So many scenarios flash before my eyes in a matter of seconds, each more awful than the last.

"Springer," I whisper in a voice laced with defeat. "I'm..."

He makes his way back to me and cups my face. "You promised, remember?"

I shake my head in denial. "No."

"Enora, this is the only way."

I grab his shoulders, unwilling to face the reality of our situation, of what it means to keep my word. "Springer – I can't."

"Yes, you can. Do it for Bram. For me."

Tears spill from my eyes. I know that once he acts, I'll never see him again. "Please."

"I love you, Enora." He kisses me hard, lips pressing against me in goodbye, calloused hands framing my head. I think his tears mix with mine, but I'm too heartbroken to be sure. Springer pulls away and stands quickly, ducking my attempts to stop him.

Leaving the cover of the hiding place, he steps into the harsh sunlight. Turning back to me, he says, "Run."

I want to scream at him and refuse, but I don't. Instead, I steel myself against the pain and dart to Ander. Hal is ready with my pack. I sling it onto my back and reach for Ander's hand. The boy is silent, seeming to understand the severity of the situation. Our only hope is to run as far from here as possible and get to that crevasse. If we're lucky, Springer will be able to misdirect whatever is coming, giving us a chance. I begin running, tears streaming down my face with each step.

My feet pound against the cracked earth, this unforgiving rock that cares nothing for the pain in my heart. Ander's hand is filmed in my sweat as we zigzag through sickly bushes and mounds of packed dirt and rocks.

Despite the speed of our escape, I'm cognizant of the need to keep to the shadows and brush. Our only chance to outrun anything will be in our ability to remain undetected.

Before long, my chest is heaving, and my body is covered in a layer of perspiration that only serves to drain my energy even more. My mouth feels sticky. My throat and nasal passages dry as a bone. I know I won't be able to keep up the pace. I'm just not recovered enough. I look around anxiously as my leg begins to shudder in spasms of agony, desperate to find a hidden spot where we can take a break. With a rush of relief, I spy a crevice between two rocks and lurch toward it, holding tight to Ander's small hand. I push him in front of me, waving my hand to shoo him to the farthest spot, in the deepest shadow.

Gasping, I fall to my knees in the dim light. It is only then that I realize we're alone. "Hal?" I gasp, afraid to project my voice beyond our refuge. "Ander, where's Hal?"

Before he can reply, we see our jeep go by. As it passes, I think I see Hal turn his head in our direction, but he's too far away for me to be sure. I know he can't see us, but I raise my hand as if I can stop him. And then he's gone, moving down the mountain. I know that when he's spotted, he'll lead the patrol away from us. For a few minutes, I sit there in silence, trying to process what just happened. The electric hum of DMC vehicles grows in the stillness until they sound as though they are right on top of us, though I know we are far from the road. I shrink back, trying to burrow into the darkness, and watch as two Company jeeps drive by single file. I don't know if they've spotted Hal yet, but it's only a matter of time.

"Where'd Hal go?" Ander's little voice asks.

I look at him, mouth partly open in astonishment over what's happened. "Um," I can't think. Oh, God. They'll kill him when they catch him. What did he do? "He went to get us some supplies." I bite my lip and return my gaze to the horizon. I can no longer hear the sound of engines, the dust is settling from the passing vehicles, and it's so quiet.

"When's he coming back?" Ander says, tugging on my shirt.

"I don't know."

I collapse onto the ground, my mind spinning. Footsteps reverberating against the hard earth interrupt my thoughts, and it's with a cry of relief that I see Springer jogging by. With a cracked voice, I shout, "Springer!"

He locks his legs, sliding in a cloud of dust, and twists his body to find me. I stumble out of our hiding place and find myself wrapped in his arms. The sobs come, and I don't stop them.

CHAPTER TWENTY-FIVE

Hal doesn't come back. His absence leaves a hole, and it's with a sense of resignation that we gather ourselves together and prepare to leave the security of our temporary sanctuary. It's only been a couple of hours since everything fell apart, but it feels like ages. Ever mindful of the chance that DMC Sentinels could descend on us at any moment, we quickly take stock of the supplies we have in my pack. What we end up with is pitiful. And foreboding. I don't let myself dwell on it, but it's there, this niggling worry. We're going to have to find a way to restock, and I'm at a loss as to how we can make that happen. Our only hope is that the area around the lake has some edible plants and such that we can scrounge until we find a town or something. At least water won't be an issue.

When Springer slings my pack onto his back, we pass

around the last water bottle and take small sips to coat our parched throats and revive our depleted bodies. I hold the bottle for Ander, too nervous about letting him have it and potentially spill a few precious drops. He drinks less than me and indicates he's had enough. It's a cruel reminder of what he is.

After looking over the options for reaching the ravine, we decide to take a flatter route. It's a bit longer, but my leg just won't let me do anything too strenuous at this point. Hopefully, we can make it by nightfall, get some rest, and then finish our journey in the morning. If we're lucky, we'll make it to the lake just after sunrise.

The sun beats down on us as we trek through the wasted landscape. Springer takes point, using his watchful eyes to monitor our surroundings. He must know how weary I am, in spirit and body, because he doesn't push me. Ander is also quiet, lost in his thoughts.

A couple of hours turn into three, and I feel the effects of the day's events in every pore. While there is a deep sadness at Hal's sacrifice, the selfish part of me is filled with such relief that it shames me. Springer is here, with me. He's not off somewhere surrendering himself, so I can escape. It isn't goodbye.

I don't speak these thoughts. It makes me uncomfortable to be so insensitive regarding Hal. But the feelings are there. I could've gone on without Springer, but it would've been just a shell of who I am if I did. And when this journey was all over, and I found the lake and given the world hope, I would've wanted it to be over. A future without him just isn't something I can face.

Springer trots toward me, stopping a couple of feet away and giving me a once-over. I'm beat, it's written all over me, and there's no hiding it. "Let's rest for a bit. There's a good spot just up ahead."

I smile. "That obvious, huh?"

"Considering your stride has gone from decent to barely upright, yeah. It's pretty clear we need to stop, or you'll drop where you stand."

I take a swing to punch him in the arm but miss and wobble. Damn. My leg feels boneless. The pain has gone so deep that I'm almost numb to it. He takes my arm to help me keep my balance.

"What's wrong with Enora?" Ander pipes up.

"She's too tired to keep walking. Think we ought to let her rest?"

Ander cocks his head. "Yeah. She could take a nap. Maybe when she wakes up, Hal will be back."

I wince when he says this, but don't bother correcting him. Neither does Springer. It's just easier that way. I let myself be led to an outcropping of rock. Crouching down, I crawl into the shade and lie on my side, a sigh escaping into the quiet. Ander scoots next to me, his small body nestling into my back. I hear Springer settle close by. Despite the intense thirst that makes my throat feel inflamed and painful, it doesn't take long for me to drift off.

The late afternoon sun casts an orange hue over the landscape when the first helicopter comes into view. They must have caught Hal and know we're on the mountain. I feel panic as it begins a slow circle. Springer looks at me with a raw expression. There is nowhere we can hide. If we leave this spot, they could see our movements. So we keep still and watch the aircraft, although I know that it's pointless if someone in the helicopter is using infrared. Thankfully, they don't seem to know where we're headed as the craft doesn't make its way any closer.

It's a relief to finally see the helicopter fly in the opposite direction. Hal must not have told them everything. Otherwise, they would know the route we are planning to take. It comes back twice more, going farther up the mountain along the logging road before it finally leaves. Shortly after, a patrol follows, driving slowly along the road, searching the sparse landscape. I know it'll be hours before we can leave our hiding spot. We'll end up traveling at night, and I worry about the rough terrain and my ability to keep up.

Despite my best intentions, exhaustion and grief take their toll, and I end up falling asleep again in the heat of the afternoon. When I wake, it's dusk, and Springer slumps against a boulder, chin resting against his chest. I can hear a Sentinel patrol somewhere on the mountain, but their voices sound so distant that I'm not concerned. I offer up thanks to Hal, wherever he is. I can't imagine what they've put him through. To know that he's been able to resist and keep things hidden, along with probably giving false information, is humbling. I wish I could have known him better.

I get up, grimacing in painful stiffness, and tiptoe past Springer. I want him to get any rest he can. I make my way to his pack and pull out a couple of our provisions, stuffing one in my pocket as I head to Ander, who is hopping from rock to rock, playing some game where he can't touch the ground. My instinct is to pop open the water bottle I'm holding and guzzle the entire contents. I suffer an internal battle as my hand shakes, physically fighting the urge to give in. I manage to keep myself at a gulp before capping it. It's hard to offer it to Ander. I watch as he brushes it away, either too intent on his play to bother or not needing any water at all.

Trying to keep him busy so Springer can nap, I join his game and pretend to enjoy it. But inside, I'm a ball of worry. There is so little water left. We've been stingy with it, but even those measures haven't been enough. Food is the other issue, but I'm less worried about that one. Living with a stomach that is always cramped with hunger has been our way of life since leaving the Company. I do worry about Ander, though.

Not having any experience with kids, I wonder if we're not giving Ander enough to keep him going, to keep him strong. What if he gets sick because he's too weak? I look hard at him. He's a compact little kid, not fat or anything, just packed with muscle in a tiny frame. Does he look skinnier? My brows wrinkle in worry. But as I see his muscles flex with each leap from rock to rock, he seems unchanged. While I don't want to give myself a false sense of security, I can't deny the relief I feel at his rather normal appearance.

"Ander, come on over and eat something." I watch as he bounces his way to me, a bundle of energy. It's exhausting just watching him romp about when I know that very soon we'll be hiking for a few hours tonight.

Grabbing the half of a protein bar I hold out, he tears into it and gobbles the entire thing in under a minute, a tactic to get back to his game. "Geez, Ander. Slow down, or you're going to get a belly ache."

"I don't get belly aches!" He cheerfully calls out and scampers off.

"Don't you want to take a sip to wash that down?" I ask, holding out the bottle of water again.

"Nope. Not thirsty."

I leave him to his game and walk to Springer. While I worry Ander's not getting enough to drink, I'm also relieved that we can ration our supply more strictly.

I nudge Springer's foot, and he jerks awake. "Sorry. I didn't mean to startle you."

He wipes his hands over his face to clear his head and straightens. "What time is it?"

"Just after six."

"Wow." He blinks his eyes a few times as he says this. "You got some food and water? I'm parched."

I let him have a few minutes to enjoy his respite and then broach the subject that's worrying me. "I don't think we've got enough food to last us more than another couple of days, and that's using it sparingly. Most of the stuff was still in the jeep when Hal took it."

"Yeah. I know."

"I don't know what we're going to do, Springer."

"I know." He rises and shakes the fatigue from his legs before continuing. "I think we need to be realistic about the real purpose of this journey."

"Okay," I say, but I'm a bit confused.

"The whole point of taking off is to show people what the DMC is hiding and to give them hope for the future. When we somehow share the location of the lake and people face the truth about how the Company has been hoarding this resource for their own use or for Ander's kind or for whatever reason they concocted, they'll rise up. The resistance will finally have the numbers they need to force the DMC to relinquish control."

"You really believe that?" I hate to even question how people would react, but the hold the Company has on everyone seems unbreakable, especially after the minimal results of the recent uprisings. It's hard to imagine so many people willing to risk everything no matter what they see.

He looks down at me. "Yes. I have no doubt. Just think about the measures the DMC has taken to keep the water hidden and out of everyone's hands, all the lies that have been told, and the sacrifices we've all had to make. And for what? So they can save it for some super-race? In fact, why even create the Aurora Strain? There must be another agenda, and I can't help wondering if it's all about control."

He's right. Covering up the existence of a constantly renewed water resource is the biggest, most awful lie the Company has told us, even worse than Ander's mutation because it signifies that the DMC isn't trying to preserve resources for humanity. "Do you think the resistance will fight for control of it?"

"I would think so. But then, there may be many groups fighting for it when we somehow show the world."

I feel a deep level of satisfaction with the idea.

Springer finishes with a final thought. "We will see this through and face the consequences of our actions when they come. For better or worse, we've gone too far to turn back now."

I agree, giving him a tight smile. How we get the truth out there is going to be a challenge, and what happens after may not be in our hands, but with any luck, our journey will show us the way to true freedom.

CHAPTER TWENTY-SIX

I carefully tip the bottle, resting the rim against my bottom lip so that I can catch every drop that trickles out. This is the last of our water. I try not to panic as I think about that. We've been walking all night. Well, I've been doing a lot of tripping and falling, my leg having gone out repeatedly as we've traveled through the narrow ravine. As dawn breaks across the sky, I release some of the stress I feel. We're almost there. The frightening searchlights of the helicopter that sent us scrambling into a dank cave during the night are gone, that aircraft refocusing its efforts in a different location.

In less than an hour, we will be at the base of the mountain on the other side of the border, a place Bram and I never imagined we would ever truly reach in our childhood musings. Despite my exhaustion, I feel energy pour through me. The end is so close.

"What do you think it'll look like?" I ask Springer.

He smiles and turns to me, grabbing my hand to keep me steady as we step over large rocks. "A deep blue that stretches for miles."

"Yeah," I say with a wistful look. "And there will be all kinds of trees all around it, types we've never seen before."

"I don't know about you, but I'm planning on stripping off these grungy clothes and jumping in."

I wink at him. "You can follow me in."

Ander comes over. "Whatcha talking about?"

Springer scoops him up, having noticed that he's lost much of his pep during the long trek. "Enora and I are going to jump into the lake the moment we get there. Do you want to jump in too?"

"Yeah! Can I splash you?"

"Only if I get to splash you back!" Springer tweaks Ander's nose, resulting in a fit of giggles. Shifting the weight of the boy, we continue, peppering the hike with talk of the lake.

We come out of the crevasse still lost in visions of water. I stop in my tracks as soon as we clear the narrow passage. We're no longer in the U.S. It's such a crazy thought. When Bram and I dreamt of a place where water ran free and clear, I always knew they were just dreams, intangible things I would never really live to see. Yet here I am, because of him. Somehow, he managed to make our dream come true. I just wish he were here to share it with me. Unbidden, tears well in my eyes as I think about everything we've gone through to get to this point.

Memories of my parents fill my mind, not their awful deaths but the good times. I think of Safa and her crazy passion for growing things. And Hal, so selfless, just wanting to be a father again. I wonder how different everything would be if we lived in a world where the DMC didn't control the very resource we cannot live without. Water. Our currency. Our lifeblood. That thing rationed and divvied out in a way that has more to do with status than need. The one resource we have been told is all but gone. That is a lie that has shaped our world, and now we can expose it.

Despite our exhaustion, there is a sense of elation as we begin the final leg of our journey. Having found some reserves of energy, Ander bounces ahead to grab hold of Springer's hand. I watch him smile down at the boy and can't help grinning. I pull out the map again to verify our location and coordinates and then scan our surroundings to get my bearings.

My voice cracks with dryness as I call out to Springer. "We need to bear right just beyond that outcropping of rocks. The lake will be in a valley about half a mile away. We should have a good view of it when we get closer."

Springer stops, waiting for me to catch up. "I want our first glimpse of it to be together." There is deep meaning in his expression.

"Together," I say, taking his other hand. Fingers

linked, the three of us hike through a foreign country with purpose.

Half an hour later, I'm practically giddy as we near the precipice that overlooks the valley. Hand in hand, we smile at each other as the horizon expands, providing a view that encompasses miles. But as our feet root themselves at the edge of a steep decline, my heart sinks as disbelief washes over me.

There is no sound aside from the wind and our breaths as the minutes pass. Our hands are no longer joined, realization having weighted our bodies until that contact was too much to bear. No matter how many times I look at the map, it still tells me the same thing. The lake must be *here*.

Drained in body and spirit, we head into what should be a verdant valley, teeming with life. Inside my mind, I've tried to convince myself the map was wrong, the coordinates off. But as we reach the valley floor, all we see is a huge expanse of what must have been a breathtaking body of water. I watch Springer walk onto the lakebed, looking down at the cracked earth, perhaps hoping to see some sign of water buried beneath the surface. I stand on what may have been a shoreline, unable to take another step. It has to be here. Only it isn't. The idea of it is just a mirage. It's a dream.

I feel weak in my body and mind. We have come so far, risked so much. It's hard to give up and face reality.

"I don't know what to do," I whisper, my throat feeling like a patch of scorched earth.

Springer, shoulders drooping with the weight of exhaustion, rubs his face before responding. "There should be a town a few miles from here, right?"

I squint my eyes at a map that is strangely out of focus. "Yeah, just east of here. A place called Verity."

"Then let's take a break and walk at night for a bit, as long as we can. It'll be easier when the sun's not out."

I'm too tired and heart sore to argue. "Okay."

"Ander, let's get moving," Springer calls out, his voice scratchy.

I watch the boy jog over, kicking a small rock like a ball. "We gonna get there soon?"

"Yep," I say with more pep than I feel. "We're going to find a spot to take a long nap for a bit first. Then we're going to go on a night hike."

"Yay!" Ander squeals and hurries over to Springer so he can walk up front with him while I lag behind.

Somehow, we manage to drag ourselves across the dried-up lakebed to the edge of what must have been a forest a hundred years ago. The trees I imagined are long gone, swallowed up in the cracked earth. Finding a shaded area under a clump of bushes, we all stretch out for a nap.

There is only one protein bar left for our evening meal. Springer breaks it into thirds and hands me my portion. It's hard and stale but should look appetizing despite that since I haven't eaten since the morning. But I'm only vaguely hungry. That should bother me, but it doesn't. My bigger worry is how I'm going to choke it down with the little spit I've got left in my mouth. I decide to nibble, forcing each morsel into my stomach. There is no relief when I finish, only a desperate thirst.

The heat of the day is gone, making it more bearable to be here, but I don't know how I'm going to manage another few miles. My leg is a throbbing, pulsing thing, laced with a pain so deep that I can't escape it. I don't know if I'll even be able to stand up, much less walk.

Ander interrupts my thoughts. "Can we go on our night hike now?"

He makes me tired just looking at him. Here I am, so weary that I can barely muster the energy to eat, and he's unfazed and ready to hike.

Springer stands slowly, his struggle evident in his sluggish movements. "I'm ready to go if you are." He says, but I plainly hear the false perkiness behind the words.

Ander reaches toward me. "Come on, Enora. Let's go!"

I roll to my knees and bend one leg for leverage. Trying to stand, my bad leg goes out, and I fall hard on my hip. Springer comes over and lifts me up, holding me until I can stand on my own.

"Thanks."

"You okay?" He asks. "You don't look so good."

"I could say the same to you," I tell him.

"Yeah, I guess you could. Let's get going. We'll put in a couple of hours, and that should take us halfway there."

I agree, and we slowly make our way through the darkness. We'll make it to Verity. We have to. I hope no one there turns us in.

Eighteen hours later, each step I take feels like a dull blade is piercing my leg. My feet drag in the dry ground, creating furrows. The sun, that merciless orb, drenches me in waves that are slowly sapping what little strength I have. There is no water. No food. No town of Verity. All that's left of that place are tumbled-down buildings sagging under the weight of dust and neglect.

Springer is no better off. With each hour that passes, I see him becoming increasingly lethargic. How many water rations has he skipped? I feel panic flutter in the peripheral of my thoughts, but I can't capture what it means. All I seem to be able to do is focus on putting one foot in front of the other. I keep my head down, concentrating on each small gain I make.

When Springer stumbles, it takes me a full minute to realize he's on the ground. I yelp in fear, my throat so dry that it comes out as barely a whisper. Staggering, I make my way to him, falling on the ground in a clumsy heap by his side.

"Springer?" My voices cracks as I shake his arm. "Hey." I shove harder, but there's no response. "Springer!"

Feeling mounting desperation, I lean over his prone form and grab his shoulders, putting all my force into a jarring motion to rouse him. All I get is a low groan. His eyes don't even flutter.

I shift into a sitting position, concentrating on lowering my rapidly increasing anxiety. Okay, I think to myself. He just needs to rest. We'll find another town, one that isn't a shell sitting out here in the wasteland. Someone will help us, give us a little food and water. We just need a little. We just need to get our strength, and then we can figure out where to go and what to do.

The day wanes, and I pass out for a chunk of time, only coming out of it when Ander taps my shoulder. "Enora," he whispers, leaning into me to get close to my ear. "Wake up."

My eyes are so slow to open. It's like they are weighed down with sand. "Ander? You okay?"

"I'm hungry. Can I have this?" He shows me a small handful of broken crackers that must have fallen out and ended up in my pack at some point.

"Sure."

As he eats, I force myself to sit up and am rewarded with a wave of dizziness. When I can see without the world tilting, I look around for Springer. My heart sinks when I see him in the same position as before. Fearfully, I pull myself over and rest my hand on his chest, breathing a sigh of relief when I feel a slight rise and fall.

I sit next to him, watching as the sky turns pale pink with the setting of the sun. Another day is gone. Springer's breathing is too soft, too shallow. I think back on all that's happened leading to this moment and realize that the journey must come to an end. All things do. Life has taught me that.

I look over at Ander, this child who is oblivious to the effects our privation has had on Springer and me. It's as I'm watching him that pieces of a puzzle seem to fall into place. Here I sit, my body wasting away from heat, exposure, exhaustion, and thirst. But Ander? He shows no signs of it.

How much water has he consumed over these last few days? Half what Springer and I did? Less than half? And there he is, happily playing by himself, healthy, vigorous. The truth, the real truth, rushes over me like a wave—like that body of water I will never see or experience except in my imagination.

This world will never get better. That was just a lie I was told, one I wanted so much to believe. There won't be a return to the old days when water fell from the sky and rivers flowed through the vastness of this nation, of the world.

I look down at the inside of my wrist and run my fingers along the raised bump I've had since birth. As I stroke my flesh, I remember what I was told not too long ago. The DMC can no longer track me. My signal has been scrambled. But if the hardline is cut, there's a failsafe, and they will be alerted. I will be traceable. We will be found.

I lean over, reaching into Springer's belt clip, and pull out his knife. Using the tip, I burrow it into my skin, digging under the microchip that has been my lifeline until recently. The pain feels good. It means I'm still alive, still aware of who I am and what I'm doing. With a quick jerk, I pull it from my body. It's such a tiny thing.

Blood oozes out of the wound in a steady flow. I watch it for a while and then lie on my back, arm resting against Springer. Though I heard nothing, I know the alert went out. They'll come for us now.

I drift into unconsciousness as I wait, awakened when I hear the drone of approaching helicopters. Too weak to rouse myself, I look up at the darkening sky, listening as the sound draws nearer. My blood has stopped its slow trickle from my wrist, the small puddle having seeped into a dry earth that sucked it up like a thirsty monster.

I let my head roll to the side on the hard surface. I can see Ander now, sitting in the dirt. I take in his deft, little fingers moving through piles of small stones, organizing them in some kind of structure that escapes me. As I watch him, oblivious to the forces that have brought Springer and me to our knees, it's so clear. Ander's kind is the only form of humanity that will survive this world. A truth that bleak compels secrecy. *This* is what the DMC couldn't tell us. There is no hope, just as there is no hidden lake in a part of the world where rain washes away the past and fills us with a promise for the future.

The aircraft touch down close by, sending swirls of dust through the sky. I ignore it. Concentrating on the realization it has taken me so long to face. A part of me shouts in anger that maybe it didn't have to be this way. Maybe I wouldn't be facing this reality if things had been different. But I can't live in a fantasy. I don't live in a dream.

Long before I was born, people made choices with unimaginable consequences. I don't know who may have been a voice of reason, who may have issued a warning of things to come. I will never learn if there was anyone who spoke for the unborn future. But even if there was one voice who fought against a tide of indifference, no one listened until it was too late.

I LIVE IN THE AFTERMATH, AND MY TIME IS over. *Our* time is over. In the end, I must accept this burden of truth.

SOME THINGS MUST REMAIN HIDDEN.

SOME SECRETS HAVE A PURPOSE.

AUTHOR'S NOTE

When I began to write this novel, I always knew how it would end. In fact, I wrote the last scene of *Burden of Truth* first. It is this scene that shapes the story. The cover of the book is when Enora looks at Ander as he's playing in the dirt and realizes that the world will never be the same, that humanity cannot survive the damage of its past. As she looks at him, she finally accepts that he is the future. That is the truth the DMC was hiding – humankind will not survive this world as it is. And now Enora is part of the layer of secrecy that will hide that reality.

The ending, however, is not meant to be an omen that our race is doomed. Rather, it is a wake-up call for the part of earth's history that we are living in this very moment. We have the power to learn from our mistakes and make changes that will preserve our planet for our species, for all species. Enora is able to look back at the choices people made, and the signs they ignored, and she knows that her life could have been so very different.

Ander is an important character in the book as he represents the future of humankind, though not as evolution designed us. His mutation reflects various research I conducted. I wanted to know what traits animal species had in order to survive in ecosystems that had little water. From that, I needed to consider which of those traits would be most beneficial to a human and would also result in a being that isn't so different, on the outside, from what we are today. I find it fascinating to learn how some species survive in inhospitable parts of the world. My focus was on mammals and I ended up selecting traits primarily seen in rodents and amphibians as the basis for the Aurora Strain (*this name was chosen specifically as it means dawn or a new dawn of humanity – Renascence also denotes this as it comes from the word renaissance which refers to a revival or renewal).

After the Green Withered began the story of Enora Byrnes, a young woman living in the aftermath of a world torn apart by global drought. In the sequel, she leaves the only life she has ever known and comes face to face with what it means to live beyond a controlling power that provides communities with everything they need to survive. The idea of a group of people rebelling against the powerful is not a new concept. The difference is that the world in this story has been so damaged that living beyond those resources means an incredible struggle on a daily basis. Enora doesn't quite understand those hardships until she is thrust into that life.

I wanted to highlight the disparities in two very different societies while also acknowledging that there are motives of those in control on both sides. It takes the harshness of experience for Enora to see that all is not black and white – those resisting the DMC are not necessarily altruistic simply because they are fighting a power that seems to keep humanity under its thumb. In the end, she sees that the DMC has a motive that isn't evil. They have simply known what needs to be done and have executed that vision with cold indifference. It is when Springer and Enora have learned that there is no hidden lake and are heading to Verity that they are forced to face the truth of their world. Verity means truth.

Throughout the creation of this book, I have had the loving support of family and friends to get me through the ups and downs of the writing process. They are my true inspiration and without them, I would not have been able to write this novel in record time—for me at least.

I want to give special thanks to my husband and three sons. I have taken many weekends and long evenings during the workweek to craft this story and each of you have been instrumental in enabling me to keep writing and fulfill my dreams. I also want to thank my coworkers who are the founding members of my tiny fan club. Vanessa and Christina—someday we'll find that red carpet! Lastly, I give huge thanks to my editor, David

Taylor at thEditors.com. Once again, you have taken something that had a good foundation and helped me bring it to life.

And to my mom, you always believed in me and wanted to read every word I wrote. I wish you could've read these.

ABOUT THE AUTHOR

Kristin Ward is an award-winning young adult author living in Connecticut. A science and math teacher for over twenty years, she infuses her geeky passions into stories that meld realism and fantasy. Kristin embraces her inner nerd regularly, often quoting 80s movies while expecting those around her to chime in with appropriate rejoinders. As a nature freak, she can be found wandering the woods - she may be lost, so please stop and ask if you see her - or chilling in her yard with all manner of furry and feathered friends.

She is often referred to as a unicorn by colleagues who remain in awe of her ability to create or find various and sundry things in mere moments. In reality, the horn was removed years ago, leaving only a mild imprint that can be seen if she tilts her head just right. A lifelong lover of books and writing, she dreamed of becoming an author for thirty years before publishing her award-winning debut in 2018.

Her first novel, **After the Green Withered**, is one of many things you should probably read.

To learn more about the author and sign up for her newsletter visit kristinwardauthor.com